A Cowboy's Perfect Match

SWEET VIEW RANCH
BOOK EIGHT

JESSIE GUSSMAN

Contents

Acknowledgments

Cover art by Julia Gussman
Editing by Heather Hayden
Narration by Jay Dyess
Author Services by CE Author Assistant

~

Listen to the unabridged audio for FREE performed by Jay Dyess on the Say with Jay channel on YouTube. Get early access to all of Jay's recordings and listen to Jessie's books before they're available to the general public, plus get daily Bible readings by Jay and bonus scenes by becoming a Say with Jay channel member.

Chapter One

"My mom called again."

Joanna Clybourn paused as she fingered the wrench in her hand. She knew what her best friend, Stonewall, was trying to say, and she knew what she was going to do, but she didn't want to.

"Here's the half-inch wrench." She handed the wrench to Stonewall underneath the tractor and adjusted her light so he could see as he lay on the ground and looked up, fixing whatever he'd figured out was wrong with it. She didn't really pay attention to those kinds of things. She was more the animal person. Which was part of the reason she and Stonewall made such a great team. When it came time to work with animals, he became her helper, just like she was his helper now.

"She's being pretty insistent. I don't want to go back to Wyoming, not for a day, let alone a month like she's asking, but...she's really putting the pressure on."

"Your mom knows how to put the pressure on," Joanna said with knowledge born of experience. Stonewall's mom had never really cared for Joanna, and sometimes Joanna wondered if she even cared for Stonewall. Stonewall always preferred the Clybourn house over his. It was a lot more peaceful, even though there were fourteen people living in it before her parents died.

"Thanks," he murmured as he took the wrench and fit it to a bolt with a couple of clanks.

Joanna was grateful that it wasn't her lying on the ground. Even though it was unseasonably warm for North Dakota for the end of March, and the snow was all melted, the ground was still damp, and he had to be getting wet through his jeans and sweatshirt.

Still, Stonewall didn't complain. He never complained. Whatever work there was to do, he did it, and they had fun while they worked together.

She couldn't think of anyone else she'd rather work with. That included her siblings, as much as she loved them all.

"Then I guess you're going to have to go," she said, saying the words lightly and simply.

She didn't want him to go, didn't want him to leave the farm. She knew if he asked her, she'd be going with him, in a heartbeat. It wouldn't be a difficult decision, but she didn't like to leave the farm either. They'd struggled with a lot of different things since they moved to North Dakota, and this year, the farm had finally broken into the black. She wasn't quite sure exactly how it happened. She suspected it had something to do with Tobias and some sort of windfall he had gotten, but she hadn't been privy to it, and no one really said. Regardless, farming was fun if there wasn't the threat of not being able to pay the bills over one's head all the time. That was the problem, other than the never-ending work—the idea that the full days of endless work didn't allow them to make enough to pay the bills.

The clanging stopped, and Stonewall's head moved out from underneath the frame of the tractor so he lay on the ground looking up at her. His face was highlighted by the glare of her phone, and she was sure that the light reflected off hers as well, even though dark had long since descended on the prairie.

"I'm not going to go without you." He said that firmly, and there was not an ounce of room in his statement for any kind of argument.

She smiled. "I wondered."

He snorted. "You did not. There was never a doubt in your mind that I was going to go without you."

She grunted. He was right. There was just an unspoken agreement between the two of them. They didn't go anywhere without the other. Whatever Joanna did, Stonewall was right there, and whatever Stonewall did, Joanna was right there. Her family had long since accepted it, and so would she. There wasn't a person in the world whom she would rather be with, and even though she had a huge, close-knit family, Stonewall was the person she'd spent the most time with over the years. He knew her better than anyone and had been her best friend as long as she could remember.

He leaned back, and she adjusted the light as he began to work on another bolt. She couldn't see his dark eyes, but she didn't have to to be able to imagine the concentration on his face, how they would narrow and he would purse his lips as he focused on his task. His dark hair was close cropped, but when he let it grow, it curled a bit at the end and looked cute curling out under a ball cap.

He currently wore a sweatshirt and jeans, which was his normal outfit on the farm, and that, along with his boots, clothes he wore naturally, looked casually handsome on him. She teased him over the years about how girls stopped and stared at him, but he never seemed to be interested in anyone.

"So are you coming?" he finally asked as he handed the wrench back. "I need a three-quarters."

She dug in the box until she found one and handed it back as he murmured a thank you.

"Of course. If you have to go, my family will just have to understand." She had a little bit of money saved up she could live on, and if they were going to be there a month, she might be able to find a few odds and ends jobs to earn a little something. She didn't have too many bills, since she and Stonewall lived on either side of a duplex that sat on the ranch property although out of sight of the regular farmhouse. The family didn't charge them rent. It just came with the fact that they worked on the farm.

"Do you think we could really leave for a whole month?" Stonewall asked, continuing to work, but his voice held the uncertainty she felt.

"Both of us know this is a terrible time. It's the middle of calving season, and with Sondra and Claudia both due to have babies any time, they're going to be out of commission."

"I know."

Neither of them said anything for a while. Their silence was just as comfortable as the conversation.

"I feel like it's selfish of me to even suggest that you should go."

"You didn't suggest it, remember? If you're going, I am too."

He chuckled. "Some people wait until they're invited—"

She smacked his calf that stuck out from underneath the tractor and was the only place she could reach. "Very funny. I don't recall inviting you to move with us from Wyoming to North Dakota."

"You couldn't live without me, and you know it."

"Maybe I couldn't wait to get rid of your sorry rear."

He scoffed. "I'm pretty sure you didn't even give me a chance to decline. It was basically, 'Stonewall, we're moving to North Dakota, get your bags packed.'"

She laughed along with him, because they both knew that was pretty much true. While she would say that they were both very considerate, they also could assume that if something needed to be done, the other was going to help.

"You know my family doesn't understand how we don't get tired of each other."

"That's funny, because the last time I talked to my mom, she assumed that I had gotten tired of you too. I think she thought I would be moving back within a month."

"It's been years. I bet she's disappointed."

"That's why she's parading Whitney under my nose. She determined that the two of us are destined to be together forever."

"I can't believe that she doesn't see that you and Whitney would never be good together." The idea that Whitney Singleton was even close to being what Stonewall needed was laughable. It wasn't that Whitney was a terrible person. She wasn't. She was actually very nice, which was probably part of the reason Stonewall was having such a hard time refusing his mother. He didn't want to hurt Whitney's feelings, and there wasn't anything bad he could say about her that was also true.

The problem was, he just wasn't the slightest bit interested in her, although his mother didn't accept that as an excuse.

"She's too perfect. She would make me feel...like I'm a terrible person."

"That's why you have to hang around someone like me. I'm so terrible I make you feel good about yourself." Joanna had plenty of sarcasm in her tone, and Stonewall didn't have a problem hearing it. They chuckled together.

"No. You're just different enough from me that we work well together, but not so different that I have no clue what you're thinking or feeling or saying. The way I do with Whitney. She's a total mystery."

"I thought men liked mysteries," Joanna said, shifting the light as he seemed to strain to look to see if he had everything together.

"Maybe some guys do. I don't know. Whitney just doesn't hold any appeal to me at all."

"Why don't you tell your mother that?"

"I have! Over and over again. But she keeps insisting that I need to come see her because she's changed, and if I love my mom, I will do this one small favor for her, and she guilt-trips me until I can hardly stand it."

"I don't think our parents should have to guilt-trip us in order to get us to want to see them."

"No. But if she had been a better mom... I don't mean that. She did the best she could." Stonewall closed his mouth.

It was a sore subject for him. There had been a lot of times growing up he felt like his mom didn't care about him. There were a lot of things she could have done to have made it better, but it wasn't like she was neglectful or a bad parent, and Joanna knew he thought she had done the best she could.

"You're right," she said immediately as he handed her the last wrench and began to slide out from underneath the tractor. "You owe her a visit. It's been what? Five years since we moved from Wyoming?"

"We've been there to see her two or three times since then."

"It's been two years since our last visit," Joanna said softly. She wasn't trying to guilt-trip him. He had enough of that from his mom.

But even though his mom had never been very kind to her, she had always tried to encourage Stonewall to do the right thing by her. After all, she assumed that someday she would be a mom, and she would want whoever was giving her child advice to advise them to at least visit once in a while.

She hoped she would be a better mom than Stonewall's mom had been. A mom like her own mom.

"Why couldn't my mom have been like yours?" Stonewall said, having slid out but just lying on the ground, like he was in no rush to get up and like the ground wasn't damp and cold.

Joanna set the last wrench in the box, closed it, and then leaned against the tractor tire so that she was sitting beside Stonewall as he lay there.

"Sometimes I wonder why I had such great parents? Like, it wasn't really fair for me to have awesome parents and for someone else, you, for example, to have parents who weren't quite as good." She was quiet for a moment. And then she added, "But I lost mine. Surely even if they hadn't been that good, there would still be a hole?"

"Yeah. That's what I remind myself when I don't really want to go see my mom. Someday I won't have her, and no matter what she's done, she will always be my mom."

"Yeah. I guess I was thinking that things even out eventually. Maybe you didn't have great parents, but you had them for longer than I did. And my parents were really good, but we didn't have a whole lot of money."

"Money doesn't buy happiness," Stonewall muttered, quoting the old saying.

"I know you're right. But sometimes it can buy peace of mind."

They sat in silence for a little while, then Stonewall said, "Sometimes I think these are the best years of my life."

"For now. But someday you'll get married and have kids and a family, and those are going to be the best days of your life. Then your kids will grow up and you'll have the house to yourself with your wife, and those will be the best days of your life. And then the grandkids will come, and those will be the best days of your life." Joanna smiled at the thought.

"You're always a glass half full kind of person."

"Most of the time, you are too. But you seem a little melancholy tonight."

Stonewall drew in a deep breath and then blew it out softly. Finally he said, "Maybe it's because of my mom's incessant nagging, but... Will I get married? Will I have children? Will I have grandkids? I guess I used to think so. You and I used to say that to each other. But that was back when we were teenagers, and the world was wide open ahead of us. But now that we're in our mid-twenties, I've started to think maybe I'm not going to get married. Or maybe my mom's right. Maybe I should give Whitney a chance. I..."

"Your biological clock is ticking?" Joanna said, not making light of what he was saying but lightening the conversational level. The idea of Stonewall moving to Wyoming and getting married to someone and possibly staying there while she had to come back to North Dakota had sent panic streaking from her neck to her toes.

"Is that what this is? I thought we're trying to figure out whether the things we've always told ourselves are actually true? And whether my mom might be right."

He sounded like he couldn't believe she might be but was willing to give it a shot.

"I guess that's another reason for you to go. To try and see. After all, there's no question that she loves you and wants the best thing for you. Of course, she thinks the best thing for you is for you to be with her, so keep that in mind." Joanna wanted to give him the advice that she thought would be best for him, but she also knew that his mother could be manipulative.

"I don't know. I guess I don't feel a great need to get married and settle down, but I can't believe how quickly life has passed just in the last ten years. It seems like yesterday we were getting our permits and learning to drive, and now here we are, looking pretty hard at the underside of thirty."

"Lots of people wait to get married until they're in their thirties. Look at Ezra, he was almost forty."

"Ezra is special. There aren't a lot of men like him in the world."

"I can't disagree with you," Joanna said, nodding her head. Even

7

though he probably wasn't looking at her. The sky was alive with stars, bright and twinkling and stretching as far as they could see into the horizon. They could be contemplating them, and if they hadn't been having such a serious conversation, they probably would be pointing out all the constellations they knew. "You are a lot like Ezra," she added, just in case he didn't know that.

"Really?" He sounded surprised.

Joanna looked down at him. Surely he knew how much she admired and respected him?

"Yeah. Absolutely. I mean, Ezra has fifteen years or more on you, but you always seemed a little more mature, a little wiser, than your age. But yeah. You and Ezra have an awful lot in common."

"Like what?" Stonewall asked, and Joanna didn't think he was fishing for a compliment. He sounded truly baffled, like he had never given it a thought before that she might think that they were alike.

"You're both mature beyond your years and always have been. I mean, I make you laugh, and Ezra didn't really have anyone like that."

"True. Ezra is more of a loner than I am."

"You're part of our big family, but you are kind of a loner apart from us."

"It doesn't feel that way."

"Ezra wasn't that way either, outside of us."

He grunted, and she assumed it was in assent.

"You're both smart, and you both think things through. That's why we're sitting here talking about whether or not your mom might be right and whether or not you should be concerned about getting married. Those are the kinds of things Ezra might have thought about, only—" Her voice trailed off.

"Only your parents died, and Ezra was more concerned about making sure the family didn't starve, and he didn't really have time for such frivolous pursuits."

"Like I said, we all have different things, different trials and hardships in life."

"That probably grew him more than anything else that ever happened to him."

"Yeah."

They lapsed into the silence for a bit, comfortable and easy, as the wind blew around them, over the North Dakota prairie, cool, but not with the biting cold of winter. The air seemed to hold the promise of spring, anticipation and excitement and the whisper of things to come. Joanna didn't usually feel restless, but for some reason, tonight she was. Maybe it was the conversation about their life slipping away, or maybe it was the idea that she hadn't thought about how old they were getting and how fast the years had gone by and she was no closer to getting married and having a family than she used to be.

She didn't want to rush into anything, she reminded herself. It would be better to never be married than to be married to the wrong person who would make her life miserable. Her mom had said that multiple times when she was a teenager and was talking about some boy or another one and asking her mom what she thought.

Her mom never told her she was too young to get married, but she had gently guided her to make better decisions.

Plus, she had Stonewall. The idea of replacing him with a boyfriend was almost unheard of, and yet, instinctively she knew that if she was going to want to get married, her husband wasn't going to want her to be so close to a member of the opposite sex. She wouldn't want that for him.

"All right. We probably ought to get back to the house. I don't want to catch my death lying here on the ground. Isn't that your job? To make sure I don't do stupid things like kill myself by lying on the wet ground?"

"I'm slacking. Sorry about that. I'll feed you chicken soup when we get home to make up for it."

"Awesome. You have food? I ate the last of my meatloaf last night before bed."

"It's not exactly chicken soup," she said as she stood up and then held her hand out for him. He took it, and they balanced each other perfectly as he stood. "It's Thai coconut milk chicken soup. A recipe I tried, and I think you'll like it."

"You probably know what I like better than I do. Right now, if it's food, I'm putting it in my mouth."

"I think you'll savor it as it goes down, but...it is a little different."

9

"Different is good, as long as it's food." He looked back at the tractor. "Let's see if this old girl starts."

Their easy camaraderie lay between them, and it felt like the heavy subject matter had long passed. Until Stonewall's phone rang.

He pulled it out of his pocket, glanced down, and then looked at her. "It's my mother."

Chapter Two

"Hello?" Stonewall spoke into his phone as he climbed into the seat of the tractor. He held out a hand for Joanna, and she grasped it as she climbed up and sat down on the fender beside him. This was an older tractor, an easier one for him to work on, especially when out in the field like this, but it didn't have an enclosed cab, so therefore no heat or AC.

"Stonewall. I just wanted to confirm that you're going to be here on Saturday for the evening meal. I've invited Whitney, and she is eager to catch up."

Just what he didn't want. He had to go back, and he didn't mind going to see his mom. Like he and Joanna had just said, he knew that it was his duty as her son to visit her and to make sure that she was okay. However, he didn't appreciate having someone shoved down his throat and for his mom to be matchmaking. He...wasn't interested in Whitney and wasn't interested in getting interested, if that made sense.

He looked over at Joanna, who could easily hear what was going on as she sat beside him on the tractor since he hadn't started it yet. He didn't have his phone on speaker, but as he suspected, she knew exactly what was said, because she nodded her head and lifted a shoulder, indicating that whatever he decided was fine with her.

She would ask her family if it was okay, but there was no way they were going to tell her no. They might even pay them both while they were gone. It had been two years since they'd taken any kind of vacation, often working seven days a week on the farm. Both of them loved the work, and neither one of them felt the need to go anywhere else. They'd talked about it, since every once in a while, Ezra would pull one or both of them aside and say that the farm had enough money that they could take a paid vacation and it would be okay. But how could they take a paid vacation when Ezra and Alaska, his wife, and all the other siblings put in twelve- or sixteen-hour days, or even longer, especially in the summer?

Neither one of them wanted to do that. Still, he could see them offering to pay for a month's vacation. Especially now that things had seemed to turn around.

"Yeah. I'll be there." He paused, then continued before his mother could jump in. "Joanna's coming with me, of course."

There was silence on the other end of the line. Silence that seemed to scream with anger and frustration.

"She doesn't need to. Why don't you grow up and do something without her? The two of you don't need to be together all the time." His mother sighed, and it sounded angry. "I thought you would have gotten over that by now. After all, you see her every day. Surely she can let go, take her clutching fingers away from you for a little while so that your mother can spend some time with you?"

He wasn't sure whether she was insulting him or Joanna, or maybe both of them.

"Joanna deserves a break, as much as anyone. And there isn't too much I do without her. She's my best friend, Mom. You know that."

"I know her family snatched you up and dragged you away from me, and you acted like they were your family, instead of your own family. I just want a little time with my son."

The touch on his arm made him look over. Joanna's eyes were bright, her brows lifted with the question. "I don't have to go," she mouthed more than said. He didn't have a problem reading her lips.

Joanna knew him as well as anyone did, and he liked to think he knew her the same. He'd never met a less selfish person. If there was a way to put anyone else ahead of herself, she always did. And it wasn't because she didn't think highly of herself. It was because she took Jesus's command to put others first seriously. More seriously than anyone else he'd ever known.

He pulled the phone away from his mouth and leaned closer to Joanna, speaking in a low tone.

"I'm sorry she's being mean. But I'm not going if you don't."

"And I'll go if you want me to. You've worked for my family through thick and thin. There's no way I wouldn't stand beside you the same way."

He stared into her eyes, this friend of his. Someone who had known him for most of his life and who had accepted him just the way he was. She knew his flaws, knew them better than anyone. But unlike his mother, she wasn't constantly trying to fix them.

He put the phone back to his ear. "We'll be there on Saturday, Mom. In time for supper."

She huffed but didn't argue anymore. And they finally said goodbye.

He looked at his phone, seeing the green call light disappear, and he stared at it a bit. The picture was one that he'd taken of the North Dakota sunrise in spring. Joanna wasn't in the picture, but she was the reason for it, and she'd been beside him while he took it. That was the kind of person she was. The kind of person who didn't need to be in the spotlight but would be behind him, giving him the proverbial wind beneath his wings, or just there with moral support. Someone he could talk to about anything, and she wasn't going to judge him or hold it against him. She could and had seen the worst of him, and loved him— like a friend—anyway.

"I'm sorry that I cause relations between you and your mom to be so strained sometimes."

A shot of anger went through him. "It's not your fault." He took a breath. His words were short, but the anger he felt wasn't meant for Joanna.

He didn't have to explain it. She smiled at his curtness.

"I think you'll be happier once we get back and you get some supper. I don't know about you, but I'm starved."

"I'm sorry. I'm annoyed at my mom for refusing to see what an awesome person you are and for being... I don't know why she's being so rude to you."

"Maybe she's jealous. Not because I'm so wonderful, but because she'd rather have your time and attention, and you're giving it to me instead."

She was always really astute that way too. More than likely, Joanna was right. His mom wasn't being mean because Joanna was a bad person. She was upset because she thought it was Joanna's fault that Stonewall was slighting her, and instead of taking her anger out on him, she took it out on Joanna.

He started the tractor up and sat for a moment listening.

"Sounds like you fixed it," Joanna said with a grin.

"Did you ever have any doubt?" he asked, sarcasm heavy in his voice.

"Of course not. I had total confidence in your ability to figure out what in the world was wrong with it and patch it back together again."

He chuckled as he depressed the clutch and put the tractor in gear. He let it out slowly so that Joanna didn't go tumbling off the fender well. A couple of times in their younger days, before he'd gotten any good at driving tractors, she'd almost tumbled off the back when he started, since he popped the clutch instead of gently allowing the gears to catch.

"Your confidence is encouraging," he said. He didn't add that it was welcome, especially compared to how discouraging his mother was. How she looked at him and didn't seem to see anything of value, but just a bunch of stuff that needed to be fixed.

"You know she loves you."

"Sometimes it doesn't seem like it."

They were quiet for a bit, and then Joanna, who hadn't let go of her white-knuckled grip on the fender, probably remembering those times where he almost knocked her off, said, "I think some people just have trouble expressing their love and appreciation. Or maybe as a mom, she just feels like her job is to see the flaws and try to fix them. And she forgets that you need her encouragement and praise as well."

Maybe that was it. Joanna was usually right about those types of things. He was the one who was good at fixing tractors, but relationships? Not so much.

He just nodded.

"What day would you like to leave?" Joanna asked, after they'd ridden a little bit more. The sun had gone down a good while before, and it was getting chilly. He wasn't sure, but he thought she shivered as she brought both hands around her waist, hugging them to her like she was trying to keep herself warm. He definitely wouldn't have minded having a coat, and he would trade his ball cap for a beanie if he could.

"I told her we'd be there by supper on Saturday, so we could leave early Saturday morning. Unless you wanted to go Friday so that we have Saturday to do a few things before we have to show up at Mom's."

"Let me talk to Ezra and see what he says."

"What about Priscilla? I know that she's been talking about going back to Wyoming. If she'd like to ride along, that would be fine."

Priscilla had been married and had two children, but her ex-husband had gotten custody. When the family had moved to North Dakota, Priscilla had come along, but it had killed her to leave her children behind. Originally she was supposed to have her children visit in the summer and at holidays, but her ex-husband hadn't been great at allowing that.

"Thanks for suggesting it. I'll ask her and see what she says. I... I know it's been hard for her being so far away from them."

He nodded his head and pressed his lips together. Seeing her sister's struggle had been hard for Joanna. Being that Joanna was one of the youngest children in the family of twelve kids, and that her parents had died when she was so young, Priscilla had been like a mother to her, along with Priscilla's twin, Phoebe.

Now that Joanna was older, they had settled into more of a sisterly relationship, but it still hurt Joanna to see her sister struggle. Stonewall knew there wasn't anything he could do about it, but when his friend was hurt or sad or upset, it definitely affected him.

The lights of the farmhouse showed just ahead, and Stonewall couldn't say that he was disappointed. It was definitely too cold to be out dressed as they were. Normally, having grown used to North Dakota weather, he was never caught without a heavy coat, even in summer. But it had been such an unseasonably warm day and he hadn't realized that the tractor wasn't going to start when they ran out to pick it up.

"I think that's Priscilla just walking into the house. How about I drop you off there, then I'll take this thing to the barn?"

"Sure," Joanna said, shifting as the tractor slowed in front of the house.

"I'll be around. Ezra might still be in the barn," he said, checking the time on his phone. "If he is, I'll say something to him."

"That's great. And if he's in the house, I'll say something to him. The sooner we can get back to our duplex and get some supper, the happier I'll be."

"Same. That, and some heat."

"It is colder than I expected," Joanna said, tucking her hands beneath her armpits once she got both feet on the ground before turning and looking up at him.

"Go on into the house. I'll be there in a minute."

She flashed a smile and then ran in. Like she was twelve instead of twenty-five. She was definitely a woman and mature, but she still had a child's exuberance and the happy heart children often have—one that was unencumbered by adult worries or problems. Not that Joanna didn't have worries or problems, she just didn't let them affect the happiness that seemed to be an innate part of her personality. Or maybe it was just the fact that Jesus shone out of her better than He did from a lot of people.

He released the clutch slowly and turned the tractor toward the equipment shed. There were a few orphaned calves in the barn, and Ezra had been helping Joanna take care of them this winter. Perhaps he was out there feeding them now. Stonewall loved the Clybourn family, but sometimes it could get rather loud and noisy and difficult to have a conversation with someone, especially when they had something serious to talk about.

Still, he wouldn't trade that support system for anything. The idea that the whole family was still together, still working on the ranch together, was almost unheard of. But Stonewall wondered if that maybe wasn't the way life was supposed to be. With families supporting each other and being a support system rather than people trying to figure out how to make a place for themselves in some strange town that they'd moved to miles away from their parents and siblings.

Was the way modern life was really the way humans were supposed to live?

He just couldn't help but feel that it wasn't.

Not that he could do anything about it tonight, he thought as Ezra walked out of the barn, saw that he was heading toward the equipment shed, and changed direction, jogging across the open area between the equipment shed and the barn to open the door for Stonewall, so Stonewall didn't have to climb down off the tractor to do it himself.

Ezra didn't just preach to his siblings that they should be considerate and kind, he lived that out.

He threw up a hand in a wave as Ezra stood at the door while he drove by.

"I'd like to have a word, if you have time," he said, not stopping as he drove the tractor to its regular spot and then backed it in.

The door closed, shutting out the light from the house and making it pitch black in the shed once the tractor's engine was cut and the lights went out.

Then the overhead lights came on, and Ezra, holding two calf bottles in one arm, a heavy coat on and a beanie cap pulled down low, strolled over, his other hand in his pocket. Casual, but a curious expression on his face.

Ezra would do anything to give him a hand, even though he wasn't technically a part of the family. Ezra had said more than once that he certainly deserved a place at the table anytime because of the work that he'd put in. A lot of it unpaid.

But there was no place he'd rather be. He just couldn't imagine that there would be a job where he could make so much money that he didn't care whether he had good people around him all the time and got to spend all of his days with his best friend doing work he loved.

Maybe he was a fool, but he thought that perhaps he'd chosen the wiser way. He was banking his life on it anyway.

"What's up?" Ezra said as Stonewall climbed down off the tractor and strolled over to where the man waited for him.

"Not much. Other than my mom wants me to go back to Wyoming."

"That's not really new, is it?" Ezra said with a little smile. Ezra knew how much his mother hadn't wanted him to move from Wyoming, and while Ezra probably didn't know how much his mom hated the time that he spent with Joanna, Ezra was an astute man. He probably had an inkling that there were issues there.

"I suppose it's not. But the new thing is, I told her I would be there on Saturday for supper."

"You're going to stay for a while? You haven't seen her for years, have you?" Ezra said easily, readjusting the bottles under his arm and crossing his arms over his chest, leaning on one leg and striking a casual pose.

"I guess time flies by and it's easy to lose track."

"Especially when you don't want to." Ezra had a slight lifting of his lips, and his serious eyes crinkled at the corners. He wasn't really making a joke, but he understood that Stonewall didn't come from the same kind of family that Ezra had. Stonewall appreciated that in the older man. Ezra wasn't quite like a father to him, but it was close.

"That's the truth."

Ezra's lips pressed together. He didn't relish the idea that Stonewall's family was the way they were or that his mother was difficult to get along with.

"Joanna is going with you." That wasn't a question.

Stonewall nodded. "I think she said one of the tenants had moved out of one of your rentals and it needed to be cleaned out. I figured we could do that while we were there."

Ezra didn't say anything, although his eyes had grown thoughtful. "I know you and Joanna are friends, best friends, and I know there's nothing going on, but it probably isn't wise for the two of you to stay in the same house together. It just doesn't look good."

Stonewall blinked. He hadn't even considered that. Joanna was just...Joanna. "I guess you're right. But I hate to stay with my mom. She's trying to set me up with the girl that she knows, and...it will be very hard to dodge if I'm there under her roof."

"Then make Joanna stay with your mom."

"My mom isn't very nice to Joanna."

"Joanna isn't weak. And she's not some tenderfooted diva who can't stand to have anyone be unkind to her. She'll be fine. And who knows, maybe she'll win your mom over if she's given the opportunity."

Stonewall hadn't considered that. He figured it was probably true though. Joanna had a way about her that just seemed to bring sunshine and happiness wherever she went. But for some reason, Stonewall felt protective of her and didn't want to expose her to his mother's unkindness. His mother could be very caustic at times. Although, if he were to tell her that it would hurt her feelings, she would be surprised. It was too bad that she couldn't take advice or constructive criticism at least. Or give herself an honest appraisal.

"I'll see what she says about that."

"If you guys wanted, you have more than a month's worth of paid vacation coming, and while it will be hard to do spring calving without you, if you'd like to take as much of that as you want to, you're welcome."

"I know Joanna won't want to miss the calves. It's hard work, but she loves it. I do too."

"You two are made for this kind of life. And you're perfect together." Ezra paused, and then he said, "Maybe your mom thinks there's more between you, and that worries her."

"I've told her over and over again that Joanna and I are just friends."

"Sometimes a good marriage begins with a solid friendship."

Ezra didn't say anything more, not that Stonewall noticed. Did Ezra just tell him that he and Joanna should get married?

"I'm going to try planting winter wheat in the back pasture. That grass can use an overhaul, and I think if we spread a good bunch of manure, get some wheat in there, and give the ground a break, we'll plant a pasture mix later this year and we might see something really good with that."

They started talking about planting and harvesting and pasture rotation, and Stonewall put the idea that Ezra was trying to matchmake between him and Joanna out of his mind.

Chapter Three

"Burr! It's cold out there!" Joanna said as she stepped in the house, feeling the heat hit her like a wall and relishing the feeling.

"What are you doing going out at night with no coat?" Alaska said with a baby on one hip and a toddler clinging to her leg while she stirred something on the stove.

Alaska, Ezra's wife, had not seemed like the perfect match for Ezra when they had gotten married, but she had taken to being a farmer's wife like she'd been born to it, and she was one of the best mothers Joanna knew. While Alaska was probably closer to Joanna's age than Ezra's, she was perfect for her taciturn older brother. She had become a good friend and felt like a sister to Joanna.

"You'd think I'd know better, wouldn't you? But we just thought we were running out to get the tractor. We didn't realize that it wasn't going to start."

"You should always be prepared for emergencies. Especially weather emergencies here in North Dakota," Priscilla said, her voice tinged with the sadness or depression that it had had since they moved and she lost daily contact with her kids.

Priscilla hadn't originally been going to stay. Her goal had been to work on the farm and be able to show the judge that it was prosperous and her children would be better off on the ranch than they were with their dad and his new wife, who brought two kids of her own to the relationship and had been pregnant by Priscilla's ex when he left Priscilla. It had been a mess, and the whole family had wanted to kidnap the children and just take them with them, but of course, that wasn't right.

"Was he able to get it fixed?" Alaska asked as she lifted the pan from the stove and set it aside before turning to get some plates out.

Joanna walked over and reached up into the cupboard, taking the plates so Alaska could hold onto her baby and pick up her toddler.

"Thanks," she said softly.

Joanna grinned. "No problem." She pulled the plates out and set them around the table. "We did. Or I should say Stonewall did. But I held the light."

"Which is a very important job," Alaska said, nodding her approval but grinning too, because Alaska wasn't any better at fixing things than Joanna was.

"Teamwork makes the dream work," Priscilla said, although the comment lacked any sparkle. In fact, it sounded even more sad, like teamwork hadn't made her dream work. Maybe there just hadn't been any teamwork.

"Speaking of that, Stonewall's mom wants him to go back to Wyoming for a visit."

"And you want to go with him," Alaska said, and there was no question in her voice. It was something she felt was obvious.

"How did you guess?" Joanna asked.

Priscilla snorted, setting a pitcher of ice water on the table, then grabbing glasses from the cupboard.

"Anyway, we wondered if Priscilla might want to come with us," Joanna said, speaking to Priscilla's back as she stood at the cupboard, getting glasses down.

"Wow. I hadn't thought about that... I'd hate to leave the farm so shorthanded with spring calving coming on."

"I'm sure Ezra would say that he would rather you go see your kids and visit back home with Joanna than be here. Even though we will be shorthanded. I should be able to help some this year. I know I wasn't a very big help last year, but I think I learned a lot."

"You were a great help last fall, and you are a quick learner. And you're not afraid, so I do think that will make a difference, but you have all your kids to take care of."

"That's true. It does take time and effort, and I can't really take them out and tag calves with me very well."

"But Tobias and Tosha might be able to give you a hand, since Tosha's gram is out of the hospital and doing so much better."

"That's true. And he was just over this morning, although I don't know what he was talking to Ezra about. But maybe it was that he would be available more." Alaska stood in the middle of the kitchen, holding both of her children in her arms and swaying gently, rocking the baby to sleep and snuggling with her toddler.

She'd had two children of her own before she and Ezra had gotten married, and Ezra and his whole family had adopted them all as theirs.

Joanna couldn't imagine the family without Alaska now. She'd settled in and seemed like a part of them.

"Well, anyway, I wanted you to know that the offer is out there. And I assume that Ezra is in the barn, so Stonewall will be talking to him about it. I guess whatever he says you guys will be able to handle."

"If I go, I'm probably not going to come back." Priscilla spoke softly, but her words were firm. "I left them, thinking that I was going to see them a lot more than what I have. I also thought that I would be able to convince a judge to give me more time with them, but..."

Her ex's family had a lot of money, and they'd been able to hire a slick lawyer who had manipulated the truth and basically got Priscilla left out in the cold with her own children.

"I don't blame you for that," Alaska said immediately. "It has obviously been exceptionally hard for you to leave your kids, and I think your place is with them. Even though that means that you won't be here, and your absence will leave a hole that can't possibly be filled."

"Thanks," Priscilla said, not looking super happy, although a ghost of a smile crossed her face at the compliment.

"I don't blame you either. Although, I hate the idea that you might leave. That makes me...sad." Joanna couldn't describe it any better than that. The idea of her older sister being several states away, rather than right here at the farm where she could talk to her anytime, was difficult. She supposed that was the reality of life for so many people. Family didn't live just over the hill in the farmhouse, or five minutes away in town, but hundreds of miles away, and could only be seen after hours of driving. She was being dramatic, because it was easy to FaceTime or have a Zoom call with everyone. It wasn't like it was the end of the world and she would never see her again.

"Ezra's been meaning to talk to you. Maybe he'll find some time this evening or before you go. What day were you thinking of going?" Alaska asked.

"We're supposed to be eating there Saturday evening for supper. So... Friday or Saturday. Stonewall hadn't decided. I think he wanted to talk to Ezra first and see what Ezra said. But I'm pretty sure Ezra's going to say it's okay, and we can stay for several weeks or a month."

"Ezra wanted to talk to me?" Priscilla asked.

"Yeah. I'm not sure what it was about." Alaska stumbled a bit, and Joanna wondered if she knew exactly what it was about but didn't want to say.

Or maybe she had an idea at least.

"Hey there." Stonewall poked his head in the door, allowing a cold wash of air to sweep through the room. Joanna shivered. "You ready?" he asked her.

"Sure am," she said, then she threw up a hand. "See you guys tomorrow," she said as she turned toward the door, trying not to feel sad that maybe someday she wouldn't be able to say that to Priscilla. *See you tomorrow.* And she wouldn't know when the next time would be that she would see her sister.

She tried to imagine not getting to see one's own children and not knowing when one would see them again. Or knowing that it would be weeks or possibly months before she saw them again.

The idea was absolutely unacceptable.

The door opened a little wider, and Ezra stepped in as Joanna made it to the door. She wrapped an arm around him and gave him a hug. He returned it with one arm, since his other arm held two calf bottles.

"Get home safe, little sis," he said, roughing her hair a bit.

She grinned at him. He always made her feel like a kid, which she didn't mind. The older she got, the more she liked it. Although, being one of the youngest in the family the size of hers, or maybe it was just being the youngest in any family, made it kind of hard to grow up and out of that idea that one was the baby or one of the "little kids."

There was a chorus of farewells, and then she and Stonewall stepped back out in the cold North Dakota night.

Stars winked overhead, bright and beautiful, like nowhere else in the country, and she pressed her arms to herself as they walked down the walk, her eyes on the beauty above them.

"I don't think the stars look like this anywhere else in the world," she said, knowing she sounded sappy and that Stonewall might make fun of her, but he wasn't going to judge.

"I think you're right. I guess that means it's home."

"What did Ezra say?" she asked as she looked back down at the path, making sure she stayed on it since with the melting snow, the yard was a little muddy.

"He said exactly what we thought he would. Take a month if we need it. We have more than that coming. And although he hated to lose us for spring calving, we should stay away as long as we need to."

"That's awesome. Ezra is the best."

"He did say he didn't think it was a good idea for the two of us to stay in the rental together."

"Why not?" she asked, trying to figure out why that would be a problem. There were three bedrooms.

"He said it just didn't look good. I suppose he's right, although I hadn't thought about it."

"I guess you would be right. I suppose two people who aren't married staying in the same house doesn't look the best. I've had people say that you and I being in the duplex living on either side of it wasn't the best, but that seems a little bit excessive."

"He said something that kind of...shocked me." That's when Joanna realized that Stonewall's voice had been subdued the whole time.

"Ezra shocked you?" she asked, trying to remember if Ezra had ever shocked her, ever, in her whole life.

"Yeah. He did. Unbelievable, isn't it?"

She glanced over at him as they reached his pickup before she walked around to her side. He had already started it, which she appreciated. She had gotten chilled and had not been in the house long enough to have shaken it.

"So," she said as her seat belt clicked and she glanced up at Stonewall as he put his on. "What did Ezra say that was so shocking?"

"He said that sometimes the best marriages are built on strong friendships."

"Like Alaska's and his?" And she snorted. She couldn't help it. Ezra was not friends with Alaska when they got married. She wasn't even sure they could be counted as acquaintances. Although they knew each other, they hadn't known each other long. Their marriage was what had sometimes been referred to as a marriage of convenience.

"I hadn't thought of that. I guess that's kind of weird that he would be saying that when his own marriage definitely wasn't. And he and Alaska seem to have a really good marriage."

"You think he was hinting around that they didn't?" Joanna asked, watching the dark landscape go by, stars twinkling overhead out along the horizon. Ezra and Alaska's marriage seemed to be very solid, and she didn't think that he was hinting, but maybe he would've been. And she just hadn't seen it.

"No, we were talking about you and me staying in the rental together and how that wouldn't look appropriate. And I think he said something along the lines of he knew that you and I weren't like that, but then he said, and he was talking about us, that the best marriages often start with strong friendships. I don't know any friendship stronger than ours, but that's not really how I took it. It was...like Ezra was talking about you and me and friendship and marriage altogether."

Joanna sat in her seat, more stunned than she wanted to admit. Was Ezra actually hinting that she and Stonewall should get married? "That couldn't have been a hint. Ezra is not that kind of person."

Chapter Four

"We weren't able to afford it before. We got the best lawyer we could. But things are different now, this lawyer is from the city, and he's used to working on high-dollar cases. And, I might add, he never loses." Ezra snorted. "At least that's what his website says."

His sister Priscilla stood with one hand on the porch railing, one hand tucked underneath her armpit, her beanie hat pulled down low over her forehead.

They had eaten and cleared off the table. Alaska had taken the kids to get them ready for bed. Normally Ezra helped with that and loved that time with his family, but he'd asked if Priscilla would walk outside and talk to him for a bit first. She didn't seem overly interested in the high-dollar lawyer that he hired in order to help her get custody of her kids.

"Maybe they're better off without me. I guess I just feel like such a terrible person."

"Don't say that." He didn't believe in self-esteem. He believed that Christians found their identity in the Lord and being a child of God, the Creator of the universe. And in their relationship with Jesus, their adoption into His family. There wasn't anything on earth that could be better. Still, it was hard to continue to keep a positive outlook about oneself when one had been beaten down as much as Priscilla had.

Ezra wasn't sure what to do about that.

"It's true. Look at me. I couldn't keep my husband faithful, and—"

"That's not on you. That's a character flaw on his part."

"Sure. I know that. But still." She sighed. "You're a man, you wouldn't understand."

"You're probably right about that. But you can say it if you want to."

The night was quiet, peaceful. A perfect North Dakota night. It did get cold in the winter, and sometimes it felt like winter would never end, but beyond that, there was a wild, rugged beauty to the land that Ezra had fallen in love with. He would hesitate to say that moving to North Dakota was the best decision he'd ever made, but it was definitely high on the list. Marrying Alaska was first, but that was all God. He wasn't even sure he could say that he wanted to at the time. But it worked out beautifully, and that was definitely God.

So why haven't You worked things out for Priscilla?

It was hard to not wonder what in the world God was doing. It felt like He'd allowed Priscilla to be beaten down so much that she was going to lose her will to continue to get back up.

"I guess I just wonder what's wrong with me. I'm not pretty enough, skinny enough, my boobs aren't big enough, or whatever it is that men like."

Ezra tried not to flinch. He didn't want to hear his sister talk about boobs.

"And I will continue to say that none of that should make any difference. If a man has vowed to be faithful, there's no excuse for faithlessness. Or to break that vow."

"But I could've made it easier."

"You are one of the nicest people I know. You certainly have been a huge part of this family, and you are an amazing mother. There was nothing you did that made it okay for your husband to cheat."

She was quiet, and Ezra thought maybe he'd been too hard on her or too emphatic. But he knew he was right. It wasn't Priscilla's fault, as

27

much as she blamed herself. And he hated that she did. Or maybe she was just at a low point right now.

"Joanna talked to me today. She said that she and Stonewall are going to Wyoming." There was a pause, almost as though she were weighing her words and wondering about his reaction. "She said I could ride with them if I wanted to. I'm not going to go with them, because I have some things I need to take care of here, but when I go, I won't be back."

Her words felt like a hard and sharp blow to his chest. He didn't want to lose his sister. He didn't want her to not come back. But her children needed a mother, their mother. Their real mother. Not that a stepmother couldn't be a real mother. He felt like the real father to Alaska's children that she had before him. So he knew a thing or two about stepchildren, but he also knew that his children were going to wonder why their dad didn't want them. Their real dad. Why he could just walk away from them. What was wrong with them that would make him do such a thing. He'd already heard them talking about it, and he tried to nip that in the bud, but it seemed to be pervasive.

"I understand that you need to go. You're needed here, wanted here, and we love you. Just the idea of you not being here...it's hard to even think about. But that's what your kids must feel too. How you were able to move so far away from them and they don't get to see you very much anymore."

"That wasn't the way it was supposed to be," Priscilla said.

"And maybe the lawyer I hired can make a difference."

"I don't want to fight," she said, throwing her arms out before turning to face the railing and putting both hands on it. "Is that what their childhood is going to be? Their dad and I constantly fighting over who gets them? I mean, I guess it should make them feel good that we both want them that much, but shouldn't we be setting a better example? All we're doing is setting an example of fighting and litigating in order to try to get your way."

"In order to try to get your children. But I do agree with you. You want to set a better example, have a higher standard. Show that you can get along with people and you can do it with love. Aren't Christians supposed to be different?"

"Yes. That's exactly right, and that's what you've taught all your life and how you lived it too."

Ezra didn't say anything. He hadn't always done everything correctly, but he tried. With all of his heart and soul, he tried to be a Christian example to his siblings first and then, after he married Alaska, to his children, because there was another generation coming up, and how would they know which way to go if there wasn't a guide for them to follow? He wanted to say with the apostle Paul, follow me, as I follow Jesus. And he wanted them to be able to do that, without seeing him say one thing at church on Sunday, then come home and live a life that was completely different.

Had he been successful? Not always.

"Still, I always felt that the only reason he wanted custody of your kids was because you wanted it and he didn't want to give you what you wanted. I never felt like he liked them that much."

"Me either. In fact, that was probably the hardest thing to swallow, that he had never been interested in the kids until I wanted them, and then it was almost like he just didn't want me to have them, and that was the only reason he was fighting for them. Makes me sad for them."

"Same." He hated the idea. But he didn't want to encourage her to continue litigation if she didn't feel it was best for her children. But he also didn't want her to quit just because she had somehow become convinced that she wasn't worthy to be their mother full-time or to have custody. "And you love them. You love them and you want what's best for them, even to the point of giving them up if that is better for them than seeing their parents fight their entire childhoods."

"And if I do that, he's there with them every day. He can fill their heads with all kinds of lies, lies that I can't counteract, because I'm not there. And even if I go back, I'm only allowed to see them on the weekends."

Ezra's hands balled into fists, and he had to deliberately relax and take a deep breath. "The new lawyer said he thought it should be pretty easy to get the custody arrangement renegotiated. It was obviously unfair."

"And I don't want you to have to pay for it."

"I want to. I want what's best for your children, and while I agree

29

with you about not seeing their parents fight, I disagree with you about *you*. They need you in their lives. Far more than what you are. And if that means you have to move back, then... I guess that's what that means, but I would rather see an agreement where you can have them here at the ranch a whole lot more, even six months of the year." He didn't say it, but he thought that maybe her ex and his new wife might be tired of having all the kids in their house, since she'd brought two, and they'd had two of their own. Also, a relationship that had begun in adultery probably wasn't going to last. Maybe her ex and his current wife weren't getting along very well, not that Ezra would ever hope for someone's marriage to fail. But if history repeated itself, he could almost be assured that would be happening at some point, and in that case, her ex would be even less interested in fighting. Maybe she would get full custody.

"There is always the possibility that things have changed, situations are different, and that you might win this fight."

Priscilla leaned her head back, looking out at the stars and breathing deeply. "That would be too good to be true."

She didn't used to be so negative. He wondered if it was his fault that she had fallen into this trap of always thinking the worst. Or maybe it was just the experiences that she had in life that had left her convinced that she wasn't worthy.

"I know it's been a long time. I know this has dragged out, and I know it's hard to see the good in it, but there's always good. God promises that."

"I know. He'll work things out for our good and His glory. I know He promises that, but sometimes... Sometimes I just can't see it. I mean, how can He use a divorce, *a divorce*, to work things out for good? Why does He have to use sin to make things good? That doesn't seem very godlike."

"God has to use what He has, and this world is a fallen world. It's going to be sinful."

"I just don't understand how anyone could say that a divorce is somehow part of God's plan or somehow part of what God's going to use to work things out."

"I don't know how He does it, but God somehow uses sin to make good things happen to us and bring glory to Him. Look at David and Bathsheba, it was adultery, then murder when David had Uriah killed, and then her baby died. How could any good come out of that? But the next king of Israel and someone in the lineage of Jesus did come out of that—the wisest man who ever lived."

"I suppose you're right."

He walked over, putting an arm around his sister, and she leaned into him. Almost as though she were borrowing from his strength. He wished she could. Sometimes in his life, he hadn't felt strong, but God had given him Alaska to hold onto and to encourage him when he was down. To lift his spirits, to comfort him and give him peace, someone to walk beside him, and to share the joys and the sorrows, the burdens and the blessings. Priscilla didn't have anyone like that.

Lord, please, send her someone to share her life with. Someone who admires her for who she is and will love her and her children without reserve.

He wanted that for his sister more than anything.

They walked back in not long after and parted ways at the top of the stairs. Ezra was disappointed that he missed bathtime. He enjoyed spending a little bit of fun time with his children, but he got to their bedroom in just the right amount of time to ask them what story they'd like him to read and to sit on the edge of the bed and spend some enjoyable time with his children before it was time to turn off the lights. Alaska stayed, and he liked those days best, where Alaska was with him, his children were snuggled in the bed, and it felt like always peace and contentment in his home. Even if things were going poorly on the farm, even if they were struggling under money pressures or personnel problems, or if he was torn up by watching one of his siblings struggle, it just all seemed to go away when he saw his children and his wife and had them all together inside on a cold North Dakota night. Where they were snuggled in the house safe and warm and surrounded by his family.

He kissed each of his kids good night once the story was finished, and then he put his arm around his wife and they went to their bedroom.

Alaska was ready for bed before he was, and she sat with her back leaning against the pillow, watching him as he moved around the room, setting his clothes out for the next morning before turning the light out and sliding into bed beside her.

She curled down beside him, and she felt familiar and perfect in his arms.

"How did things go with Priscilla?" she asked, as he had known she would. There was no way she was going to allow him to talk to his sister and not tell her every word. Not that he could remember every word.

He stroked down her arm and curled his fingers into hers, holding her hand while he spoke.

"I know God is never late, but it kind of feels like it in this instance." He didn't want to say that he didn't have faith that God was going to work things out. He did. He just didn't understand what was taking so long.

"What do you mean?" Alaska asked, her fingers tightening in his. He squeezed her hand back before he drew his hand out of hers and settled it on her thigh.

"She is so beaten down." He tried to explain what he meant. "She wasn't even excited about the new lawyer. And she argued that she didn't want her children to grow up and only remember their parents constantly fighting and litigating, and I can't say that I blame her, but it's almost like she doesn't feel like she's worthy of having custody. Even though it kills her not to see her children."

"Everyone says she hasn't been the same since shortly after you moved and she realized that her ex wasn't going to do what he had said he would, and she wasn't going to get to see her kids."

"I know. That was a really hard blow, and I wondered if maybe I should've encouraged her to move back immediately. I feel like maybe it was my mistake."

"Don't give yourself a hard time. You couldn't know. Plus, her ex is probably ready to move on to his next woman, and maybe she'll get the kids herself. He might welcome her trying to get them."

"I actually thought about that myself. It seems like a relationship that starts with adultery isn't the kind of relationship that's going to last, and I never really liked that guy anyway."

He shouldn't have said that. "You know what I mean. I know we're supposed to love everyone, because we're all human, created in God's image, but he was a hard one to like and appreciate."

"I knew exactly what you meant," she said.

He sighed, his heart still heavy.

Alaska moved her hand along his leg which was thrown casually over hers, and he closed his eyes. "I know you take the responsibility of caring for your siblings seriously, and I have to say that what you did with Tobias and Tosha was nothing short of brilliant."

"I wasn't sure whether that was going to work out or not." He smiled, his eyes still closed.

"It did, and nicely too."

"I...might've jumped the gun a little bit, but I've been working on Joanna and Stonewall for years, and they both seem oblivious, so today when I was talking to Stonewall, I might've mentioned that strong friendships make a strong foundation for the best marriages."

He could feel his wife shaking with silent laughter.

"What's so funny about that, wife?" he said, saying the word *wife* so it sounded like an endearment. Which, he felt like it was.

"What made you think I was laughing?" she asked back, sounding saucy.

That was one of the things he loved about his wife; he felt so comfortable and secure with her that if she laughed, he never worried that it was at him, it was always with him. And he hoped she felt the same about him. They had a good time together, always.

"I suppose if you weren't laughing, I could...make you start." He moved his hand lightly over the sensitive area of her ribs. She was exceptionally ticklish there. She wiggled and squirmed, but he wasn't done talking. Or, more accurately, he knew she wasn't.

She had grabbed both of his hands, and he had allowed it, threading their fingers together and pulling her even tighter against him.

"What did he say about that?" she asked, settled once more.

He moved back through his mind, remembering that he just confessed what he had said to Stonewall in the barn about best friends and marriage.

"I think he was a little surprised, and then... I'm pretty sure he brushed it off. Whatever he did, I don't think he took me seriously, and we started talking about crops."

"That might be a good thing. You don't want your siblings to think that you're pushing them into getting married."

"When I really am?" he asked, lightly teasing.

"Because of me. After all, I'm the romantic and I want all of your siblings as happily married as we are."

"We are happily married, aren't we?" he said, wondering again at the goodness of God.

"I know. You didn't see that coming, did you?"

"It was love at first sight. I just wasn't sure I liked you."

She laughed, knowing he was teasing her. But also knowing that he was serious at the same time. She wasn't the kind of woman that he ever thought or anyone ever thought that he would end up with.

"I'm so glad that you were willing to listen to the Lord, even though it seemed like a crazy thing for Him to have you do."

"Everyone thought that. Myself included, but it was the best thing that ever happened to me. *You* are the best thing that ever happened to me."

She melted in his arms, and he figured that maybe they'd talked long enough.

"That is one hundred times more true for me. You are the best thing that ever happened to me. And can you blame me for wanting your siblings to know this? What we know?"

"What do we know? Maybe you're going to have to help me out with that. I'm a little confused," he said, trailing his fingers down her arm and then moving on to her hip and thigh.

"If you're trying to say something, you could just come out and say it, rather than leaving hints."

"That wasn't a hint. I asked you to show me. I'm waiting."

"It doesn't feel like you're waiting," she said, and he laughed, because she was right. She was quiet for a moment, and then she said, "You've done an amazing job with your siblings. Everything that you've done has been with God's glory and their happiness in mind."

He paused, his hand on her stomach. "I'd really like to get Priscilla taken care of, but I have a feeling that Stonewall and Joanna are about to find out exactly how much they mean to each other and that a relationship with their best friend might not be such a bad idea."

"I have a feeling you're right. Now, if you don't mind, I don't want to talk anymore."

He smiled. Those were some of his favorite words.

Chapter Five

"Are you packed?" Stonewall asked as he met Joanna on their porch. It was Friday evening, and they had agreed to watch Agathe's husband Jim so that Agathe could go to her swim aerobics class and get a little bit of time away from caregiving.

"Almost. What time are we leaving again in the morning?" Joanna asked as she stepped down off the porch beside him.

For some reason, rather than going to his own door and opening it, he walked to Joanna's side and opened hers.

He wasn't sure why he did it. It was right there, sure, but it was always right there. And they always just went to their own sides and opened their own doors. After all, that's what friends did.

So, the odd look she gave him was not unexpected.

"So...did Ezra give you a hard time for not being nicer to me or something?" she asked with her hand on the seat, pausing and looking up at him.

"No. All he said was what I told you he said, which I really think he was just making conversation. I...can't imagine that he was actually talking about us."

But it must've planted seeds in his head or something, since he just did this really unexpected thing.

"All right, but hey, you can keep opening my door for me. I'm certainly not going to turn it down." She winked at him and then jumped in his truck.

He laughed, shaking his head and thinking about what an idiot he was. Why did he open her door? He couldn't answer that. So, he just dismissed it, chalked it up to just one of those things.

"You never answered me about what time we're leaving in the morning," Joanna said as he got in his side.

He paused with his hand on his seat belt. "I told you like three times. And we talked about it. It's not like I decided. We decided together."

"I know, but we talked about many different times, I can't remember the time we actually settled on. Can you?" she asked as the motor rumbled to life and he put both hands on the steering wheel.

He shook his head, pretending to be annoyed, but he wasn't. This was Joanna, and she was over there, smiling, teasing him gently, but also being serious, because he knew she really didn't remember what time they had settled on. That always seemed to be his job, and he didn't mind. "We decided on two AM."

"We did not!" she said immediately.

He lifted a shoulder. "I thought you said you didn't remember."

He backed out, laughing to himself.

"I don't remember what we settled on, but I do remember that two AM was not part of the discussion."

"Then you tell me."

"I don't remember!"

"We said we'd leave at four. That way, we should miss the worst of the traffic and get there at a fairly decent hour so that we can rest a bit before we have to go to my mom's. I believe it was you who said that she was the kind of person that you didn't like to have to deal with when you were weary from traveling all day."

"I'm pretty sure you said that," she said dryly across the seat.

He laughed again, because he knew it was him. He just liked to tease her. He just liked to be with her. He just liked...her. Maybe... Maybe Ezra wasn't so far off the mark. Maybe the best marriages did begin with a solid friendship, and he definitely had that. But he knew more than one friendship that had been ruined by dating. He didn't want to go down that road, but he really liked Joanna and couldn't imagine doing things without her.

"Did you make a meal for Agathe?" he asked, glancing over and realizing her hands were empty. He'd been so busy teasing her that he hadn't even noticed.

"No. Ryland was going to do that. The library was closed today, and she and Lucas were going to spend some quality time in the kitchen together, I guess."

"Poor Lucas," Stonewall said, but he didn't really mean it, and Joanna knew it.

"I'm sure Ryland shared whatever she made with him, and that made it okay."

"Lucas would do pretty much anything for food."

"Well, the truth is he would do pretty much anything for Ryland."

"Agreed." Lucas and Ryland made such a cute couple. Lucas was so outgoing and people oriented, and Ryland was the exact opposite. They looked adorable together, and they fit together perfectly. While they didn't share any strengths or weaknesses, they did share interests, and that seemed to make the fact that they were complete and total opposites completely okay.

Maybe Joanna and he were too alike to be together.

Why was he even thinking about that?

"You seem to be driving slower than usual. Is there something wrong?"

Joanna's voice startled him. Had he really gotten that deep into contemplation about his best friend and whether or not he might want to pursue a romantic relationship with her? Especially when he never considered such a thing before in his life. People had teased them all the time about being together and they'd always easily denied it, never being awkward or anything, and now...now one casual statement from Ezra had him trying to figure out if that might not be the best idea.

"I guess I just have some things to think about."

"You need me to help you?" Joanna asked easily.

"No. I guess, my mom is a little difficult, and I don't know how to make things easier for you."

"You mean now that I've agreed to stay at her house instead of at our rental?" Joanna's head flew around to look at him so quickly he almost looked out the window to see if she was looking at something. "Did you get out of it on purpose? Did you tell me that Ezra said that we shouldn't share the rental when in reality he didn't say any such thing? You just didn't want to be stuck at your mom's, so you wanted to punish me and have me be stuck there?"

"I'm a little confused."

"You made that up about Ezra so I would be stuck at your mom's."

"Joanna, no matter what it might seem like, I really do like you."

She laughed, as he had known that she would. And then she said, "You shouldn't say those kinds of things about your mother."

He could have said she was going to say that too. He knew her almost as well as he knew himself.

"I wonder if Mr. Jim will be lucid enough to play cards with us tonight?" Joanna said. The fields outside the truck windows were starting to green up, although they would more than likely be covered with snow again before summer officially arrived. Not that it mattered. Once things started to get green, he could be patient about spring and summer. It was that promise lurking under the snow that everyone knew was there. Plus the fact that the snow melts faster in the spring.

"I don't know. The last two times we've been there, it seemed like he was going downhill pretty quickly."

"I know. I feel so bad for Agathe. The worse he gets, the worse she looks, and at this point, I wonder if it's more humane for us to just wish that he would go quickly, because she seems exhausted and completely worn out, but at the same time, she still obviously loves her husband."

"Yeah," he said. If he were with a girlfriend or a romantic partner, they might be upset with him for giving a one-word reply, but Joanna wouldn't. She knew sometimes he just didn't have words. And she gave him grace for that. But right now, he wasn't necessarily thinking about what she said, other than thinking that she was the kind of woman who would stand beside her husband through everything, including taking care of him as he aged.

But what if it was Joanna who needed to be cared for? He would happily do it. He wouldn't leave her. He would consider it his honor to be able to serve her.

That sounded more like a husband than a best friend. But...had he ever thought about kissing Joanna? Because husbands do a lot more than kiss their wives. He glanced over at Joanna.

He should have known that she was going to see that out of the corner of her eye as she glanced over at him, catching him.

"What?" she asked, looking at him with her brows drawn.

"Nothing." He supposed he probably looked guilty. And she wasn't going to accept that word for one second.

"Nothing, my foot. You look like you are sticking your hand in the cookie jar, except you're driving and I know you're not. What's going on?"

"Oh, look at this. We're at Miss Agathe's house. Wow, that ride didn't take very long at all."

She wasn't the slightest bit distracted, and he figured that she was going to be on him again before the night was over, but she let it go since they were pulling in and it was time to get out.

"We're going to talk about this, Mister." She raised her brows at him and gave him a stern look before she got out of the truck.

He had a little bit of time to try to make something up. Why would he have been looking over at her?

"I just thought you had something green in your teeth," he said as he came around the front of the truck. That was a bold-faced lie. And it didn't sit well. But he felt like he was teasing her more than anything. After all, what was he going to say, *I was looking at you to see if I might like to kiss you someday, because husbands kiss their wives, and I was thinking about becoming your husband?*

No. He couldn't say that. He definitely had to make something up. Still, lying was wrong. He could never do it without feeling guilty, which was probably a good thing.

"Do I?" she asked, pulling her lips back and showing him every single one of her eight-seven and a half teeth.

"That's a lot of teeth," he said.

"Do I have anything green in them now?" she asked, her words slurring as she kept her lips pulled back and tapped his shoulder when he started to turn away.

He figured that if he wanted off the hook, he had to follow through, so he turned back and fixed his gaze on her mouth.

By that time, she was running her tongue over her teeth, and his eyes kind of got caught on that and the way her lips moved. There was a little dent at the top of her upper lip, which gave them a bow shape, and her lower lip was full and very, very kissable.

Wait. Kissable? Joanna?

"Stonewall! Pay attention! Look at my teeth."

"How do you know I wasn't looking at your teeth?"

"You have that far-off look in your eyes the way you do whenever you're contemplating doing something that is going to get me into serious trouble."

"I've never done anything that got you into serious trouble."

"Yes, you have. It was your idea to steal those candy bars from Mom's pantry, which would've been fine, if you hadn't decided that we needed to steal all of them."

"No. Stealing all of them wasn't a problem. The problem was, you ate half of one before you stuffed the rest of them in your pants, and having half of a candy bar in your mouth as you're walking through the kitchen might not have been terrible, if you hadn't had chocolate smeared all over your face from when you shoved it in your mouth. *That* is what got us into trouble."

"Fine. You're right. I made a tactical error which I never repeated, thank you, but it was still your idea and it started with that look."

"It couldn't possibly have started with this look. I was eight."

"You were nine, and it did start with that look. That look is ageless."

"Ageless? That's like...not a word to describe a man."

"I'm not describing a man, I'm describing *you*."

They had reached the door, and she turned to knock before she grabbed the doorknob and turned it.

But he went still at her last statement, and it was still reverberating through his head. She wasn't looking at him as a man, she was looking at him as...? Did she not look at him like he was a man? Did she not realize he was a man? What was that supposed to mean?

And then he shook his head. He was a man. He wasn't supposed to ruminate over or worry about exactly what that term meant. But it was Joanna, and he wanted her to see him as a man, someone who might kiss her and she might enjoy it.

No. No. *Wait.* That was *not* what he wanted.

He'd never been this confused in his life before.

"Joanna! Stonewall! I'm so glad you guys were able to come," Agathe said as she hurried toward them, her arms out.

She enveloped first Joanna and then him in one of her lilac-scented hugs. Maybe it wasn't lilac, but some kind of expensive French perfume that her husband had bought her over the course of their marriage, and she had confided to Joanna that she had never worn it because it was expensive perfume and she was saving it for a special occasion. Then she realized that she was losing her Jim, and she wanted to wear the perfume for him, so she started wearing it on a daily basis. It was French, because she was from France and Jim had bought it for her to remind her of the country of her youth, the one she still loved, but the one she had left for the man she loved.

Stonewall had often wondered if he would have someone to love him like that, but...it just hadn't seemed like he should be in a hurry to find her, and then with Ezra's comment and maybe it was something to do with his mother's pushing him as well, he had to wonder if maybe the woman who would love him like that had been under his nose the entire time.

And if Joanna was, indeed, the perfect woman for him, would he be able to talk her into it?

Chapter Six

Agathe smiled as she left the house, her husband safe in the care of Stonewall and Joanna. Those two made such a sweet couple, although from every indication, they were just friends. She hadn't believed it at first when they moved from Wyoming and that's what she heard. After all, they were together all the time, more so than most married couples, and seemed to enjoy each other's company, and truly seemed to like each other. They finished each other's sentences, teased each other, laughed together, and were totally comfortable and confident with each other. A perfect marriage. Except... They weren't.

But it reminded Agathe so much of the relationship that she and Jim had had.

She took a deep breath of the cool North Dakota air and slid into her car, throwing her bag on the passenger seat. She hated leaving her husband, knowing that any day could be his last. The possibility that he would be alive for another fifteen or twenty years or even outlive her was there as well. But the days that he knew her were almost over. It had been just a few minutes each day since he had seemed to know who she was, and that amount of time was getting shorter and shorter.

If she continued to think about that, she was going to be sad before she even made it to the community building where her water aerobics class was held. She couldn't think about her husband and how she was going to miss him and already did. She also didn't want to think about Waylen and how she hadn't seen or heard much of him lately, since she turned him down three times in a row after he asked her to go out for ice cream with him. She felt guilty the first time she'd gone, although she had such a good time.

She didn't want to lose the opportunity to perhaps move on after Jim was gone, but... She just didn't have liberty from the Lord to hang out with a man who was not her husband.

Meeting with these ladies and doing water aerobics was part of what she did to keep herself from being lonely and depressed. It was easy to get depressed in a North Dakota winter, especially when one didn't get out much, and so she made a deliberate effort to accept the help of anyone who offered. Even when she didn't feel like it.

It was a short drive to the community building, and she got out of the car eagerly, excited to spend some time with her friends and almost as eager to slip into the water, where she felt lighter and freer, which was almost a metaphor of her life, slipping into the water, slipping out of her problems and her thoughts and her concerns and her fear for the future. What was she going to do when Jim was gone? Who was going to take care of her? They had never had children. She had no one to lean on.

That wasn't true. She had God. God created the universe, He calmed the storm with words. Surely he could take care of her.

Plus, He'd given her a whole town of people who seemed to care about her and others like her. She never had a lack of people offering to stay with Jim so she could go somewhere. At least twice a week, someone came so she could get out. And at least that many times and sometimes more, someone dropped off supper, or a casserole, or a gift card for the diner in town.

She thought for a moment about how God had taken care of her through every step of her life, and she felt bad.

I'm sorry that I don't seem to trust You no matter how trustworthy You are, Lord. You've never allowed me to go hungry, not even a day. And You haven't left me lonely either, and yet I have such a hard time giving my burdens to You and letting You carry them.

Multiple times, she'd asked God to carry the burden of Jim for her, and multiple times, she felt like she'd given that burden to Him and walked completely away from it. And then, she'd go running back to pick it up just minutes or, at the most, hours later.

That certainly didn't say much for the faith that she had. But part of her said God had allowed Jim to get Alzheimer's in the first place, and He was going to allow Jim to die, why should she trust Him? But trust didn't mean that He'd never allow anything bad to happen to her.

She knew, just by looking around at the rest of the world, bad things happened to everyone, with no preferences made. It wasn't that. Trust meant that when bad things happened to her, God would take care of her. He would be with her, and the idea that she could just simply allow things to happen because God was in control gave her the greatest peace she'd ever felt. The problem was, she didn't always remember that.

But she remembered it now. So, she reached for that peace, allowing it to settle into her soul, relaxing into the idea that God was in charge and that everything would work out for her good and His glory.

Smiling at the thought, she grabbed her bag and stepped out of the car, seeing Rhoda and Bernadine talking in the parking lot. Instead of walking into the building, she slipped her bag over her shoulder, clutching her purse in her hand, and walked over.

"Good evening," she said, looking up at the sky and wondering if maybe she should have said afternoon. It was probably only four o'clock.

"Agathe. I'm so glad you could come today. How's Jim doing?"

Bernadine really meant well, but it seemed like everyone greeted her with that question. It was part of the reason she struggled to get out. She couldn't really forget about Jim; she was reminded of him every time she met someone. But she also reminded herself that the question meant that people cared. And she shouldn't resent it.

"He's doing as well as he's been. Slowly sinking into that fog, or wherever he goes, and spending more time there every day." She smiled. "He's eating well, and he seems to be less upset and angry than he had been earlier last fall."

"I think that's pretty much a good report," Rhoda said tentatively.

Agathe nodded, appreciating the fact that she was trying not to draw inferences that were inaccurate. "Yes. I consider that a really good thing."

"I hate to be the bearer of bad news, but I'm afraid that Asenath has been told that she has cancer, and it's not looking good." Rhoda lowered her voice and looked around the parking lot like she was afraid someone might overhear her.

"This is something we're not sharing with anyone?" Agathe asked right away, because she didn't want to be the one who shared news that was supposed to be private.

"No. I don't think it's that we're not sharing, it's that Asenath is having a hard time with the diagnosis. She's supposed to be coming today, but she had her doctor's appointment on Monday, and I don't think she's been out of the house since then."

"Does she have a surgeon lined up? More doctor's appointments to figure out the treatment plan?"

"That's just it. She has it so bad that...they suggested she not go with a treatment plan but call hospice instead."

"Oh." Agathe's heart fell the whole way to her toes and hit the ground hard.

How terrible to have such a diagnosis, and especially when Asenath was barely eighty years old, and a young eighty at that. She was fit and healthy and looked good, although she'd been complaining all winter about being tired. They chalked it up to the fact that there wasn't much sun, and it often made people, especially women, sleepy and crave carbs.

"I feel terrible. She's said for months that she's been tired, and I just told her to get more of those sun lights. I never thought of telling her to go to the doctor to get tested for cancer. Maybe if she had gone last fall when she first started complaining. Maybe if I had suggested—"

"We all said that. That it was just a lack of sunlight, and she needed to stop wearing herself down so much because she was eighty years old. None of us suspected that it might have been cancer. I don't think we should have. Tiredness might be a symptom of cancer, but everyone gets tired. It's not something you can control." Bernadine patted her arm and looked into her eyes with so much compassion that Agathe figured she had probably drawn the same conclusion herself and come to the realization that there wasn't anything that she could have done to prevent it.

"But now that we know, we decided that we're going to rally around her and support her as best we can. She does have some family, and they might be coming in to help, but whatever they don't take care of or can't, we figured we'd ask the ladies tonight to pitch in and help." Rhoda gave Agathe a long look. "I know that you'll help however you can, but...with Jim, you're already a full-time caregiver, and that's exhausting. So no one's expecting you to give anything you can't."

"I want to help. I really do." It was true. She longed with all her heart to reach out to her friend and do what she could, but Rhoda was correct, how was she going to? She was depending on the help of others just to get out of her house, to go grocery shopping, to do regular chores. Thankfully someone had volunteered to mow the grass all year last year, or she wasn't sure what she would've done. Even taking an hour to sit on the lawn mower, as much as she enjoyed it, was risking Jim running away and getting lost like he had when the Clybourns' barn had caught on fire. She couldn't find him and panicked, and thankfully, while there were a ton of people helping with the barn, there were also people who volunteered to help her find her husband. They found him in the grocery store, wandering the aisles, holding a candy bar in his hand that he couldn't remember whether he had paid for or not.

He had been upset that she had been upset, saying something along the lines of, "I should be able to walk out of my house without having to tell you every little thing that I ever do. You're not my mother."

It had hurt. Because they had always told each other where they were going and what they were doing and when they thought they would be back. She thought that just meant they took care of each other. She cared where he was, and it made her feel good that he cared where she was. Like they had someone who loved them and wanted to know what was going on with them.

"Thank you for your consideration," she said finally.

Both ladies came and put an arm around her, and she leaned her head on Bernadine's shoulder. "I feel like such a burden when I want to be a blessing."

"Everyone has those times in their lives. Times where they've had an operation or they've been sick or they are caring for someone, or maybe they broke a leg. Just times where they need other people to help them. And that's when you realize that when you get the opportunity, you need to try to be a blessing to someone who needs it, because you appreciate the people who did that for you."

"I suppose there are opportunities for learning in every situation." If that wasn't one of the lessons that Agathe had learned over her life, she didn't know what was. Whatever trial God had her in, He had lessons He wanted her to learn, and she learned to just look to Him and say *what do You want me to know, Lord? What am I supposed to learn in this?* Somehow it made a fiery trial not seem quite so hot.

"And if you aren't being a blessing, that opens an opportunity up for someone else to be." Rhoda gave her a squeeze, and then they started toward the community building.

"Let's go in and share with the other ladies. And then, if Asenath comes tonight, it can be up to her whether or not she wants to share."

She said a short prayer for her friends, thanking God that He had given them to her and asking Him for the opportunity to someday be a blessing to them. But then, He seemed to whisper back that she already had been. She'd given them an opportunity to be a blessing to her, and that was being a blessing in itself.

Chapter Seven

Stonewall was acting weird. There was no other way to describe it.
Joanna sat in her seat and looked across at Stonewall covertly,
doing a good enough job that he didn't take his eyes off the highway to
look at her.

He'd opened her door again. Which was weird. She kinda laughed it
off yesterday when they were going to Agathe's, but then when they
came out of Agathe's house, he did it again. And then this morning, he
not only carried her suitcase out, but he opened her door for her again.
She wasn't even able to make a joke about it this morning, because she'd
been so...weirded out by it. That wasn't the way their relationship was.
It had never been that way, and she wasn't sure she wanted it to be that
way. It's not that she didn't like her door being opened for her. Because
she did. It was just the idea that he was her friend, not her romantic
interest. Romantic interests opened doors, friends...joked about it.

Maybe she was making too big of a deal about it. After all, that was
really the only thing that had changed. That, and he carried her suitcase,
and just...there was something off. He was thinking about something,
but she couldn't quite figure out what it was. He wasn't telling her, and
usually she didn't have to ask. Usually he would think about it until he

was ready to put it into words for her, and then they'd discuss it together. But so far, that hadn't happened.

She was still waiting, and normally she was pretty patient, but this was taking longer than it usually did, and it must be something pretty serious.

Should she ask him? She never asked him. That would mean that she was acting weird too. Maybe she should just wait and see. Maybe if she were patient... Patience had always paid off before, and she had no reason to think that it wouldn't this time too, except... She didn't want to be patient. She wanted to know what was going on.

"Are you going to tell me what you're thinking about?" she finally asked, curling her toes in her boots and trying not to act as nervous and uncomfortable as she felt. She was never nervous and uncomfortable around Stonewall. So that was weird too. All of the stuff was weird, and she didn't want their relationship to change. Was that what was going to happen on this trip? Maybe she should have stayed home. Maybe she should have tried to talk him out of going. She didn't want anything to change. Change scared her.

"What makes you think I'm thinking about something?"

"Do you really have to ask that?"

"It seemed like a reasonable question."

"I can just tell, and you know that. The same way you can know when I'm thinking about something."

"You think?"

She laughed. "I think occasionally. I'm pretty sure you've been witness to it once or twice."

"I suppose I have, and I actually like it when it happens. Rarity makes stuff more valuable, or whatever that saying is."

"You're hilarious," she deadpanned. "But I haven't forgotten that you didn't answer the question. What are you thinking about?"

There was a long, long pause. It felt like a mile or more went by before he spoke.

"I was thinking maybe it's time to get married."

She liked the silence better. But no. She wanted the best for Stonewall. She loved him. He was her best friend. She would do anything to make him happy or to make his life easier, no matter what it was. Even if it meant their relationship would change.

So, he was seriously considering Whitney. Well, she could help with that. She could do something anyway.

She took a breath, because the idea of losing her best friend made her stomach feel like sludge and her lungs feel tight and hot. But she supposed she'd known forever that this day might come. And she wasn't going to ruin his life by making him feel guilty about wanting to move on.

"I think you're right. I think you should try to keep an open mind when it comes to Whitney. I mean, I remember her as being someone really nice. In fact, if it hadn't been for your mom always pushing her on you, I would've really liked her."

"Really?" he asked, glancing over the seat at her. He didn't seem overly interested in Whitney, but he did seem interested in her statement. "You think I ought to give Whitney a chance?"

He didn't sound like he wanted to. That made Joanna feel like she needed to press him on it. After all, if she were totally sold on the idea, he might be too. Maybe he had been holding back because he was afraid of what she would think or was afraid that she would feel pushed out. Maybe she ought to start the conversation that would allow him to feel like he could leave their friendship and pursue a romantic relationship, since that's what it would take. He couldn't just pull in a romantic interest. After all, she didn't want to be with a man who would insist that she be part of a male-female relationship.

"Yes. I definitely think you should give Whitney a chance. I told you, I really liked her. It was your mom's pushing that made her odious to us. Not the girl herself." She took a deep breath and mentally tried to prepare herself for this. Why did it feel so wrong? "She's a great girl for you. And she suits you perfectly."

"You think she does?" he asked, sounding surprised.

"Yeah. I mean, she really is nice. And she's sweet. And as I recall, she wasn't pushy at all. In fact, I'm pretty sure she had a great sense of humor." Yeah, come to think about it, Whitney was pretty much the perfect girl. Beautiful, with long flowing hair and a wonderful, curvy figure. She had been confident without being overbearing and sweet

51

without being a total pushover. And she had seemed to be totally infatuated with Stonewall. Of course, who wouldn't be?

Joanna gave him a covert glance, and he seemed to be focusing so hard on the road, with his brows puckered just a bit, that he didn't even notice.

He was strong and confident, but also kind and compassionate. He was funny, and could always make her laugh, and was exceptionally loyal. He also worked hard and was honest and upright. Who wouldn't love him? He was basically the perfect man.

Of course he did have flaws. He snored for one, which she only knew because if they ever watched a movie on a Sunday afternoon, he fell asleep about two minutes after it started and snored the entire way through the movie until the end when he woke up and asked what it was about. Maybe she should warn Whitney that movies weren't Stonewall's strong suit.

Maybe Whitney wouldn't appreciate her telling her what Stonewall liked and didn't like. Probably Whitney wanted to find that out for herself and didn't want to hear it from another woman. Even if that woman was Stonewall's best friend.

But his wife should be his best friend.

What was that line in the Bible? You must increase and I must decrease? It was John the Baptist talking about Jesus, but it seemed to apply in her situation as well. It certainly wasn't right for her to expect the biggest spot in Stonewall's life if he had a woman he intended to make his wife.

And there she was getting ahead of herself. Stonewall hadn't even seen her for several years, he wasn't thinking about making Whitney his wife. But he was going to date her. Wasn't he?

"You are going out on a date with her, right?" she said, maybe as much to convince herself about it as it was to convince him. But he needed to. If he was ever going to get married, Whitney was perfect.

"I was hoping you would help me figure out how to get out of it. I don't want to."

"Why not? Whitney's perfect."

He gave her a look that she couldn't read. He didn't have too many of those. But it kind of looked like he was exasperated with her.

"What?"

"Whose side are you on?"

"Yours, of course. You know I'm always on your side."

"Right now, it feels like you're on my mother's side."

That gave her pause. Was she on his mother's side? She didn't want to be exactly, but she always said that his mother truly did love him.

"I'm not on your mother's side. But I'm on the side of people who love you. And I think she does. She just doesn't always have a great way of showing it. But introducing you to Whitney might be one of those small ways. After all, Whitney's a great girl, you said so yourself."

"I wasn't expecting you to say so or to try to talk me into dating her. It almost feels like you're trying to get rid of me."

It was on the tip of her tongue to shout, *never*! But...wasn't that what she was trying to do? Wasn't she trying to put a little distance between them so that he would see that Whitney was a great person and he should put some effort into her?

Her chest felt like little earthquake tremors were going through it, making her feel unsteady and like she needed to grab a hold of something in order to keep her balance, but she opened her mouth anyway.

"I'm not trying to get rid of you, but we have to face the fact that we can't be like this forever."

"We can't?" Now his brows really were lowered as he looked over at her. She met his eyes for a brief second before he turned back to the road. Of course they couldn't be like this forever. Why hadn't she seen that before? Seriously, both of them were old enough to get married and start having a family of their own, and they couldn't do that when they had someone of the opposite sex as their best friend.

"No. How would you feel if the girl you wanted to marry had some other man as her best friend and refused to put any distance between them, and you felt like you were in a three-way relationship, rather than the type of relationship that God wants you to have?"

He blinked a bit at that. She pressed her advantage.

"We both know this can't go on forever. If you're going to get married, if I'm going to get married. If we're going to have children. If we're going to have families. We can't do this. You being with me probably makes it look like you're not interested." She sighed. "I should've stayed home. I didn't even see that until just now."

"I told you I wasn't going to go if you didn't, and I meant that. And I feel a little bit like I need to turn around right now. What's wrong with you? We can still be friends even if I get married. But I'm not planning on getting married. I don't even know Whitney. I haven't seen her for literally two years."

His words made her feel good and bad at the same time. She didn't like that feeling. And she tried to push the good away. She didn't really want him to be loyal only to her. She didn't really want him to be alone all of his life and to give up a really great chance of being with the one he was meant to be with because she stood in the way.

"Maybe this is God working things out so that you meet the one you're supposed to be with. Maybe I should've stayed home. Maybe my presence will keep you from spending time with Whitney." She made a snap decision. "When we get there, I'm going to call one of my brothers and have them come pick me up immediately. You deserve this time to figure out whether Whitney is the one that you want."

"If you go, I'm following. I'm not staying here without you."

She turned and looked at him. His words brooked no argument. His hands were clutched tight on the steering wheel, his knuckles white, and a muscle in his jaw moved back and forth, like he was clenching it in anger.

"All right. I will go, on one condition. You have to promise me that you will give Whitney every chance possible. That you go on at least three dates with her with an open mind, and that you will try as hard as you can to see whether or not she would make a good wife for you."

He didn't say anything, and they drove in silence for what felt like a very long time. For the first time that she could ever remember, the silence between them was uncomfortable, charged, electric, but like a static electricity that made her hair stand on end and made her wish that something would come to diffuse it. She didn't know what or how. And she didn't like the way it felt. Her relationship with Stonewall had always been easy, fun, completely natural. This was not the first time that they disagreed. They disagreed all the time. But this was the first time she could ever remember that it didn't feel...casual and easy, the way the rest of the relationship felt.

"I feel like you just took all the power in our relationship and wielded it over me to make me do what you want me to do when that might not be what I want," he finally said.

She blinked. That felt very insightful, especially coming from Stonewall. He didn't typically talk about how he felt. It was usually stuff he thought and what made the most sense. She was the one who usually went by her feelings.

And after that thought came another. He was right. She had just manipulated the relationship and basically was trying to force him to do what she wanted him to do. Even though it was for his own good.

Should she continue to try to force that when he didn't want to?

"I'm sorry." She knew she needed to say that much. "I wasn't trying to take the power in our relationship." That was actually a really great statement, because it was exactly what she had done.

"That's weird. Usually you're not quite that subdued and submissive." He gave her a glance with one raised brow, almost as though he were expecting her hair to catch fire and for her to start spitting out snakes or something.

"You're right. It didn't feel right after I said it, and when you said that I was trying to force you to do what I wanted you to, it made sense why it didn't. Because you're right, I was."

"What I don't understand. Why?" He asked that question without looking at her. His eyes were fixed on the road, the endless stretch of highway that flowed out in front of them.

That was easy. "Because my thought was it was best for you. I realize I'm the one that's standing between you and the potential that you have for happiness. I don't want to be the reason that you never get married and have kids. I want you to be happy, and if that means that you have to be happy without me, I would rather make that sacrifice."

"I really can't imagine my life without you. Let's don't talk about that. If I get married, my wife is going to accept the fact that you are my friend, or there is not going to be a marriage."

"And that's what I'm afraid of!" she cried. "Men might be okay with that, I don't know. But I know that there is no woman on the planet who wants her husband to be best friends with some other woman." She sighed. "Women want to feel special. They want to know that their position in your life is unique and that there isn't anyone else who compares to them in your eyes. I don't think women need to be the most important person in the world, but they want to be the most important person to their husband."

"My wife will be." He said the words emphatically. "But she also will understand that I can have friends, and one of those friends will be you."

"I want to be your friend. You've been the best friend I've ever had. Sometimes the only friend I've ever had," she said with a laugh. She had gone through times where she couldn't seem to get along with anyone, but she'd never gone through a time like that with Stonewall. "You deserve a wife and family."

He didn't say anything, although his first finger thumped on the steering wheel almost as though he were thinking and wanted to say something but couldn't find the words for it.

She let him think. She'd apologized for what she'd done and wanted to vow never to do it again, but she loved him so much, loved him with an unselfish, friend kind of love that she wanted him to be happy, even if it meant that she had to sacrifice some of her own happiness.

She paused as a thought struck her. Was that the kind of love she loved him with?

She believed it to be so. She had said to herself that he was the perfect man and any woman would be proud to have him...wasn't she any woman?

She tried to imagine what that would entail. Holding Stonewall's hand. Kissing him. And more.

She blinked. She wouldn't mind holding his hand. He was strong, and his grip would be firm, tough, and her hand would feel safe in his. In fact, far from not wanting to hold his hand, the idea held a lot of appeal.

And kissing Stonewall?

Her fingers curled. The idea was unreal, but at the same time, she had to admit, she wasn't repulsed. In fact, if she were being completely honest, she wouldn't mind trying it out.

But no. That wasn't the way their relationship was. Stonewall had never, in any way, indicated he might be attracted to her as a woman. They were just friends. Good friends, close friends, they had the kind of friendship that only came around once in a lifetime, if that. She didn't want to ruin it by thinking that it should turn romantic. But she also didn't want to ruin it by pushing him away when he didn't want to go. That choice should be his, and he was right.

"You were right when you called me out earlier."

"You already apologized for that," he said, although his voice sounded like he was thinking about something else.

"I wanted to explain that I felt like I was doing it for your good. I don't want to stand in your way, and I won't. But the choice that you make is yours. I don't have the right, and I don't want it, to push you into anything that you don't want."

"And that's a promise," he said, and it wasn't really a question. He gave her an easy smile, and she returned it, nodding.

"That's a promise."

"Then I promise to give Whitney a fair chance. I'll go on three dates with her if I have to, although I've never really thought dating was a good idea. Your family has the best handle on that that I've ever seen."

"My family has a good handle on it because my family is huge and we can do that kind of thing. Invite people over to work with us, to hang out with us, and that way we can kind of see their character and the people they are." Stonewall had been hanging out with their family forever. She knew what kind of person he was. She knew that if a child came up to him demanding that he do something, he could handle it easily and with grace and that he didn't have a problem talking to anyone from the youngest child to grandparents. That he could change the diaper on a newborn just as easily as he could throw a ball to a five-year-old and help a teenager with their algebra homework.

Sure, he lost his cool at times, but so did she. He always apologized, was quick to apologize and admit that he was wrong.

"Regardless, more people should be like that. You don't learn anything about someone on a date. Dating is for after you're married."

"I think my family has brainwashed you," she said with a chuckle.

"They might have, but I've seen it work. You don't date to learn how people are, because it doesn't tell you anything. You bring them home to your family and then watch how they interact with people of all ages. That's how you learn what someone is. It is funny that when people want to pair off, they want to be alone. They don't want to see their potential spouse with other people, they just want to have all of their time for themselves."

"That's so true. But I guess maybe the people that are able to overcome that desire, and at least wait a little until they've observed the person and how they interact with other people, definitely win out in the end."

"I couldn't agree more. But I'll date Whitney if you want me to."

"I suppose you could bring her home to my family." She didn't know where those words came from. She didn't want Whitney in Stonewall's life at all. She definitely didn't want Whitney in her life and her family's life as well as Stonewall's life. Although, they all seemed to be intertwined.

"That might not be such a bad idea," Stonewall said thoughtfully. "I suppose if you want me to be serious about this, that's what I would do."

"Do you think your mother would be okay with that?"

"Probably not. She never thought that was a good idea anyway. She's totally about what the world thinks."

Joanna didn't say anything. She felt a little bit bad for Stonewall. His mother had definite ideas about how things should be, and she didn't like for anyone to think that she was wrong.

"What if your mother came too?" Joanna finally said as the miles slipped away.

"Are you actually suggesting that I bring my mother back to North Dakota with me?" He lifted a brow at her as though questioning her sanity. After all, his mother basically hated her, and they both knew it.

"I guess that was kind of a crazy idea."

"She probably wouldn't want to anyway."

"She could come back with us to North Dakota and work on the farm." She couldn't believe the words left her mouth. Was she arguing to try to bring not just Whitney, but Stonewall's mother back to North Dakota? What was wrong with her?

Nothing. There was nothing wrong with her. This was her better side coming out. She was trying to be self-sacrificial and do the best thing for Stonewall. Maybe this wasn't the best thing, she didn't really know, but it would require sacrifice on her part, and she was willing to make it if that's what Stonewall wanted and if it was what was best for him.

"Maybe we're getting the cart ahead of the horse. We don't even know exactly what's going on. I mean, my mom did mention Whitney and that she would be there, but we don't know that she's going to be pushing for us to date and, who knows, maybe Whitney is in love with someone else," Stonewall muttered thoughtfully. Like he was breathing it out and hoping it to be true.

"You're right. We're getting things way ahead of ourselves. But the ideas are there, so if we need to jump on them, we can."

"I'm going to assume you're saying that because you want the best for me and not because you're trying to get rid of me."

"That's the correct assumption."

He looked across and smiled at her, and she smiled back, and she felt like the little wobble that their relationship had had been restored. She had caused that wobble, and he had called her out on it, and she was glad he had. After all, if he had gone along with her and the rest of her ultimatums, she wouldn't have respected him as much, and she might have been completely wrong.

There was a small part of her that said she might have been completely right too, and maybe that was worth considering. But not worth ruining the friendship she had over it. And she needed to remember that.

Chapter Eight

Stonewall spent the rest of the ride trying to figure out what in the world had gotten into Joanna. It was like she wanted him to have a girlfriend, to get married, and to have a family. Like she wanted to be rid of him.

So funny, because he had just decided that maybe he wanted *her*. And she had, apparently, just decided that she wanted to be rid of him. It hurt his ego a bit, but it hurt his feelings more, and it hurt his heart the most.

It wasn't exactly something that he was proud of that it had taken him this long to realize that his best friend might actually be the best person in the world for him to marry, and that holding her hand and kissing her would not be a hardship. They were so familiar with each other that they almost acted like an old married couple anyway. He couldn't imagine walking through life with anyone but Joanna.

But he promised her that he would give Whitney a fair chance. Maybe she was right, and actually, she had to be right. If Joanna wasn't interested in him, if he was going to get married, he needed to find someone else.

What about Joanna, though? Did she have someone in mind? He searched through his brain, trying to think of all the people who showed up at the ranch on an almost daily basis. The guy who delivered feed, the mechanic who came when no one in the family could figure out what was wrong with the tractor. Folks who came because they heard that the ranch had been successful and they wanted to see. Tourists who came to stay at the dude ranch in the summer. Folks in town. There were lots of different men her age who weren't married and were probably looking. Guys who lived on various ranches around the area, including the Sweet Water Ranch, or the truck driving family and the family who owned the auction house. Sons and cousins of those people. Good, hard-working men who might turn Joanna's eye.

Was she trying to get rid of him so that she could pursue a relationship? Was that why she gave him that story about how women want to be special? So that he would ditch her in order for her to be able to be with some guy, because he hadn't said, but a man didn't want to share his girl with anyone. He wanted her to be the sole focus of his life. Right after Jesus came the woman that he pledged his life and love and heart and soul to.

They didn't have time for those kinds of conversations, and he wasn't sure he wanted to have that with her anyway. Because he wasn't sure he wanted to know that she already had someone in mind.

Once they hit Wyoming, he had a fairly good idea of which way to go, and he turned off the GPS. It was two hours later, after they stopped to get gas and a bite to eat, that he pulled up to the Clybourns' rental that had just recently been vacated. This was where he was going to stay. But he and Joanna had already agreed that they would both stay here for the afternoon before going to his mother's this evening. They both knew that if he went to his mother's, she would want him to stay and would be upset if he went to the rental. It would be easier to do that this evening after supper.

Regardless, they were both tired from being up so early and from their hours of travel.

"Well. The yard needs to be cleaned up," Joanna said as he turned the motor off on his pickup.

It was a rental in the small town of Fullness. Her parents had bought it as an investment, back before they had a pile of children and no money. They had planned that it would give them income in addition to the ranch, and it had, but it also needed regular maintenance and upkeep, which was hard to do from North Dakota. Her brothers had suggested they hire a property manager, but they were a little bit difficult to find in this area of the country. The town was small and wasn't exactly brimming with rentals and property managers.

"If that's how the yard looks, I'm kind of afraid to see the inside."

Joanna nodded beside him, quiet.

"I guess when I said that I would come to take care of the rental, I assumed that maybe a few things would need a new coat of paint, and perhaps a door would need a hinge. But I'm guessing there's going to be a lot more than that going on." Her voice was subdued from the other side. And it made him realize that they hadn't talked about the main purpose of their visit at all. Which was getting this rental ready to have new tenants.

"Maybe it won't be bad. Maybe they just took everything they didn't want, and maybe they couldn't fit everything in the moving truck and left the stuff they couldn't use out in the yard."

"Yeah. Those empty beer cans probably aren't something they were going to need at their next home," Joanna said, grinning at him, and it was a small glimpse of her old self. There had been something off with her ever since she had given him that ultimatum. Like she decided in her mind that she needed to sever their relationship, and he didn't want to look into it any more deeply than that, because then he went down the trail he'd been on before with the thoughts of another man and Joanna having a family without him, life without Joanna, life without his best friend. It seemed bleak and hopeless, and he didn't even want to contemplate it.

"All right. Maybe I'm a little off the mark. But there's no point sitting out here and being all gloom and doom. Whatever it needs, we can handle it, and we will. Let's go find out exactly what that is."

"I needed a pep talk, thanks." Her laughter echoed as she opened her door and jumped out of his truck.

He should have gotten out and gone around and opened it for her. He'd never done anything like that before, and even just him going to the door and opening it up for her to get in had made her look at him funny. But he should have been doing it all along. Although if he had been doing that all along, maybe they wouldn't have stayed such good friends.

Maybe the relationship would have become more. Maybe she would have seen that...she was the one he wanted.

The idea was still fresh and new, and he wasn't sure that maybe the idea of not having her had made him want her more. Wasn't that a human nature thing? A person wanted what they couldn't have?

That wasn't the way he wanted to be, but maybe that was the way he was, and he just hadn't realized it, because the idea of not having Joanna definitely made him want to hold onto her tighter.

But holding onto her tighter would only make her want to struggle to get away more. That was the nature of things. That was the way it went.

He jerked the latch on the truck and followed her out of the truck. They stood at the bottom of the porch steps together, looking up. There were several boards missing, and there was trash littered all around. It must have been this way for a month or two. He couldn't remember when the tenants had moved out.

"They've been out for six weeks. It's looked like this for six weeks."

"I can't believe no one's complained," he said, glancing up the street. The houses weren't exactly neatly kept, but they were well kept. Obviously it was Wyoming, a small town, and no one here was rich by any stretch, but they were good people who tried to do their best, and that included keeping their trash picked up and their house looking as good as they could.

Joanna pulled the key out of her pocket and started up the steps. "I guess we might as well do this now."

Ideas of lying down on a couch for a small nap disappeared. He didn't even know what he was thinking about that. There might not be any couch. Although Joanna and Ezra had both said that the furniture had been conveyed and the house had been rented as partially furnished and some of the furniture was theirs.

They expected that the tenant would have left it when they left, but somehow, Stonewall's mind told him that what they had assumed might not be accurate.

63

Joanna put the key in the lock, and it clicked. The town was quiet, and the click sounded loud in the fresh air.

There wasn't a stoplight or a grocery store in the town, and the streets were deserted this time of day. Probably everybody was at work and school.

Joanna pushed the door open, and Stonewall watched as the room became visible.

He slowly let out a breath. It wasn't nearly as bad as what he had anticipated.

The house looked clean, if not swept, and there wasn't any trash lying around.

"Maybe teens have been having parties in our yard since no one was here to tell them not to," he said.

"That makes sense. And since it's a small town, everyone would have known that the renters had moved out and no one had moved in."

"Now that we're here, that should stop."

"I think you're right."

As they looked around the house, things weren't terrible, but Stonewall was glad that Joanna had agreed to stay at his mother's house. If his mother would allow her to stay. He hadn't even thought to ask if it would be okay with her if Joanna stayed in his place. How had the potential of her exploding all over him missed him?

That question was easy to answer. It was because he wanted what was best for Joanna, and staying with his mother seemed like it would be.

There were several beds and mattresses left upstairs, and with the mattress protectors and sheets that they brought they were able to get a room set up for him to stay in. The leather couch downstairs had seen better days, but Joanna had brought several blankets and was able to wrap herself up in them and take a nap.

Stonewall went to his room, but he didn't sleep. Instead, he lay on his bed, hands behind his head, staring at the ceiling.

Obviously there had been some activity going on outside the house, and he definitely did not feel safe having Joanna here. He was licensed to carry and often did, but he hadn't brought any weapons with him. Now he wished he hadn't made that oversight. But once Joanna was out with his mom, he would feel better. Wyoming usually felt like a very safe place to him. But he supposed that places could change, demographics shifted with new people moving in and out.

He tried to think of any time that Joanna had given any indication that she might be interested in him as more than a friend, but after their conversation on the way here, it was hard to even picture her acting in a romantic way toward him. She had pushed him so hard at Whitney, had crossed lines that they had never crossed before just to try to get him out with someone else, that he wasn't sure what to make of it. Other than to accept the fact that what he had all of a sudden decided that he wanted wasn't in her mind at all.

But it had taken him a while to decide that it was what he wanted. Up until Ezra had said what he said, he had never considered Joanna in that way. Not that other people hadn't said that they looked like boyfriend and girlfriend or mistaken them as romantic partners, but somehow it was Ezra's words that finally pierced through to him and got him to actually open his eyes and see what was right in front of him. *Joanna.*

He could expect that she would be the same as him. Completely blind and a little oblivious to what could potentially be between them. Maybe he just needed to be patient and work on cutting through that blindness, until he was able to make her see that they would be better off together. That they didn't need a different romantic partner. That best friends truly did make the best marriages.

Of course, he didn't know that was necessarily going to be true for them. Maybe they would make terrible romantic partners. But he was of the mind that once a man made vows, he could be faithful to whomever he made vows to. Same for a woman. That it was less about romantic love and more about the type of person who would make a commitment and stick to it. He was certain he was that way, and he knew beyond a shadow of a doubt that Joanna was that way as well.

Chapter Nine

J oanna tried to settle the butterflies in her stomach. Going to Stonewall's mother's house always made her feel nervous and insecure. Dixie just had a way of making her feel like she wasn't good enough, and most of the time, it wasn't overt. Her words just basically said that Stonewall could do better than hanging out with Joanna all the time.

Stonewall gave her a look, almost as though he were bolstering his courage too as they both stepped up the walk to the door. He rapped once and then twisted the knob. It was unlocked.

He held it for Joanna to walk in first. She wanted to protest, to say it was his house, and his mother, and he should go first, but she stepped in calling out, "Hello, the house!"

"Mom! We're here!" Stonewall called behind her, and she appreciated that so much. He wasn't feeding her to the lions. He never had. He was always right there beside her, usually with a grin and a look that said he was having the time of his life.

That was typically when they were outside doing something, whether it was riding horses together or four-wheelers or swimming in the river. This felt like a completely different kind of danger. More intense. More insidious.

She tried to shake the thought. It was Stonewall's mother, and Dixie was not a bad person. Just because Dixie didn't care for Joanna didn't mean she wasn't good.

"Hello!" A woman entered the room, not Dixie. It must've been Whitney, although she'd grown up since Joanna had seen her last. She was beautiful, with long wavy hair, and she wore a flowing white blouse along with jeans that weren't exactly tight but definitely showed off her curves. Her feet were bare, and somehow they gave her a sexy look that seemed natural and unaffected, but still extremely appealing, and that was just Joanna's take. She could only imagine how Stonewall was affected.

But she wanted this. She wanted Stonewall to look at Whitney and see a woman that he could spend the rest of his life with. After all, unless Whitney had changed, she was a great person.

"My goodness. It's only been two years, but I don't think I would recognize either one of you. You both have done a lot of changing in the last few years," she said, hurrying toward them. "Stonewall and Joanna, right?" she said, her laugh tinkling a little, her words light and fun, as though of course she knew who they were but she just wanted to make sure since they were so different.

There didn't seem to be any kind of underlying meaning in her speech, and Whitney walked forward, a smile on her face, her arms out.

Joanna mirrored her action, and they ended up embracing.

"Yes, it's Joanna, and I am so happy to meet you again."

"Wow. You are more beautiful than you were before you left." Whitney stood back, staring into her eyes, and Joanna got the impression that she was being honest. Whitney thought she was beautiful?

"She does grow more beautiful every day, doesn't she?" Stonewall said thoughtfully. That made Joanna's brows draw down. What was he doing? He didn't think she grew more beautiful. He didn't even think she was beautiful to begin with. Was he playing some kind of game?

She looked at him, but Stonewall gave her a gaze that held no guile and then looked back at Whitney.

"You're just as lovely as you used to be as well," he said, holding a hand out which Whitney ignored as she walked toward him and hugged him.

Joanna did not miss the tightening of his lips as he accepted her hug, patting her on the back gingerly before pulling away.

Maybe it was just her imagination, but Whitney seemed to cling just a little longer than Stonewall wanted her to.

"Oh, you're too kind. When you have a raging beauty like Joanna with you every day, any other woman would have to pale in comparison." Joanna did not get the feeling that Whitney was just saying words. "Your mom's in the kitchen. She sent me out to greet you and to bring you in."

"It smells good in here," Stonewall offered as Whitney turned around and started walking. He indicated for Joanna to go first, and to her surprise, he put a hand on the small of her back as she moved in front of him.

He was touching her, which wasn't completely unusual, but he didn't typically touch her like that. And it felt...good and right but odd at the same time if that was possible. Maybe, just unusual, but not bad.

"Your mom is making all of your favorites. It should smell good."

"It's not just me making them. In fact, I've been doing a lot of standing on the sidelines while you cook, Whitney." Dixie spoke as they walked into the kitchen, wiping her hands on a tea towel and hurrying over to embrace her son.

Joanna noted that the woman did look older. The lines about her face had deepened, and new ones had appeared. Her hair was more gray than brown, and she added some pounds onto her frame.

She still looked matronly and confident, and outside of her treatment of Joanna, she seemed like a nice person. She definitely was happy to see her son, and she clung to him and said, "I can't believe it's been two years since I've seen you. You need to come back more. In fact, you need to move back. I don't have a whole lot of years left."

"Don't be ridiculous, Mom. You're just in your fifties. You have another several decades of good life left. Plus, you wouldn't want me underfoot all the time. I was always annoying you."

"I was never annoyed." She huffed indignantly as she pulled back but held onto his arms so she could study him, looking up into his face and beaming. "You look better than you did when you left. Definitely working outside agrees with you, you're strong and hard and very handsome. If I do say so myself." She turned a beaming face to Whitney. "Isn't he?"

Whitney's cheeks pinkened, and Joanna did not envy the woman her position. "He's very handsome."

That's all Whitney said, but it sounded sincere, and Joanna felt the sting of disappointment. She wanted to not like Whitney; she wanted Whitney to be a bad person. She wanted there to be something that she could latch onto to say that Stonewall should stay far away from Whitney.

But wait. No. That's not what she wanted. She wanted Stonewall to have a good wife. Whitney seemed like the very best woman Stonewall could possibly have. She should be rejoicing in the fact that Whitney seemed to be fresh and sweet and young and kind and absolutely dear.

Except, there would seem to be a part of her that didn't. That actually wanted Stonewall for herself. But that was selfish. She couldn't give Stonewall a good life. He wasn't attracted to her that way. He didn't want her as a wife. He didn't want to create a family with her. It was wrong of her to want him when he had no interest in her.

"All right, you go ahead and sit down, and we'll finish up the meal." Dixie dropped Stonewall's arms and started to turn away.

"You didn't greet Joanna, Mom," Stonewall said, and there was an edge to his voice that hadn't been there before.

Joanna tried not to take offense. After all, Stonewall's mother was just going to completely ignore her existence. To pretend like she wasn't even there. Talk about rude and unkind. But Joanna tried to remind herself that Dixie loved Stonewall, and she felt like Joanna was in the way.

"Hello, Joanna," Dixie said coolly.

"Hi, Miss Dixie. It's good to see you again. You look well." There, saying it was good to see her again might've been a bit of a stretch, but saying that she looked well was absolutely true. Older, but good.

Dixie nodded her head and then beamed at Whitney before she turned back to the stove. "Whitney just completed her master's program at Cheyenne University. She's a certified reading specialist, and she's considering getting her doctorate degree. I have to say it's been amazing to watch her work and earn her degree in just a little over a year. She's quite diligent when she sets out to do something."

"You make it sound like I did something special. People do this all the time. And I was a schoolteacher. I have a free period at the end of the day and I can get most of my grading done then, so I have the evenings to study. It wasn't that hard," Whitney said, looking embarrassed, indeed, at the praise that Dixie had heaped on her. "You were always a very good worker too, Joanna."

Oh goodness. Not only was she sweet and kind, but she was going to be sweet and kind to Joanna to try to make up for what Dixie wasn't doing.

"Thanks. I guess there does need to be some kind of diligence inside of you in order to stick at farming, even when it doesn't seem profitable."

"Which is pretty much all the time," Dixie said over her shoulder.

Dixie had been a schoolteacher, so it made sense that she would be partial to schoolteachers. Maybe that was the issue, since Joanna didn't have a degree next to her name. She had stayed to help her family on the farm instead. She thought that was more beneficial to the people around her, although maybe it wasn't as beneficial to herself, but she didn't care. She knew that wasn't the way the rest of the world thought, but she had been content with her decision.

But maybe Dixie had been upset that Stonewall hadn't chosen to go to school either. Probably because Joanna hadn't.

In fact, Joanna remembered his mom being completely upset, now that she thought about it. But she and Stonewall had made the decision together. It wasn't like she had made the decision and not given Stonewall a choice. They hadn't wanted to be separated, and they had known that her family needed help. It seemed like a reasonable choice to stay and help.

"Is there anything I can do to help?" Joanna said as Stonewall sat down at the table, telling her with his eyes to go ahead and sit down too.

"No. We've got it under control," Dixie said as she added a sliced stick of butter to the potatoes before turning on the mixer to mash them.

Whitney came over and put a hand on her shoulder. "You guys have been driving all day. Just take it easy for a little bit. You could help clean up if you want to."

Whitney's kindness truly did help to ease the sting of Dixie's obvious dislike. She could only imagine what Dixie was going to do when she found out that she and Stonewall had decided that Joanna was going to stay with her.

She smiled up at Whitney. "Thank you." She meant *thank you for your kindness as well as letting me know that I can rest a bit before I help.* But she didn't say that.

Chapter Ten

Stonewall wanted to grab his mother by the throat and shake her. How could she be so mean to someone he thought so highly of? Maybe his mother didn't actually care about him, or she'd care about people that he cared about. But he knew that wasn't true. His mother truly did think that she was doing what was best for him, even though she was doing it in an unkind way.

He remembered Ezra and all the brothers, including Caleb especially, commenting about how important it was to think the best of others.

Caleb was probably the best of the Clybourns at doing that. While Caleb wasn't the oldest, was stuck in the middle somewhere, fifth or sixth in birth order, he had been the one that Stonewall had been closest to over the years. Maybe because he had always seen the best in Stonewall and always been the first to extend an invitation to a stranger. Not that any of the Clybourns were reluctant to do that.

It seemed prudent to apply that to his mother if he was going to apply it to anyone and to try as hard as he could to see the best of her. Regardless, he wasn't going to allow her to treat Joanna badly.

His mother turned the mixer off, and conversation was possible once again.

"I hope you're going to stay for a while. You did say that you were going to take Whitney out, and she's been so looking forward to it. We went shopping for clothes yesterday, and I had so much fun."

Whitney looked embarrassed that his mother was talking like that, although she didn't deny that they had gone shopping for clothes.

"It's so much fun to buy new things. And it's even more fun when you know you have an event you can wear them to," Joanna said.

"I was talking to Stonewall." Dixie turned, her eyes hard as she allowed them to bounce onto Joanna and then off again.

Stonewall stood so quickly his chair toppled over.

"Joanna is my friend," he said, his voice low and level and didn't hint at the fury that seethed within him. "You will be nice to her. Or we will leave."

His calm, soft words lingered in the kitchen as everyone froze.

He knew he was making Joanna extremely uncomfortable. She didn't like it when he made a scene, and she certainly wouldn't want a scene to be made about her, but he needed to nip this in the bud, or it was going to go on through their entire visit. He was not going to spend a month watching his mother being unkind to his best friend.

"I didn't realize I wasn't being nice," his mother said, a little defiantly, lifting her chin and her brows as though daring him to contradict her.

"I don't think I need to give you a lesson on what being nice is. And I think you know exactly how you were being. It needs to change, or we're out of here. As much as I love you, and as much as I want to spend time with you, don't think I won't. And I'm also willing to go out with Whitney." That sounded terrible. If he were Whitney, he wouldn't want someone who said that he was *willing*. "She seems like a really nice girl. I remember her as being such. I would love to get to know her better. I would love to go out on a date with her." There. That should solve that problem. "But I will not if Joanna is not treated with respect and kindness in this house." He could almost hear Ezra's voice echoing in his head as he said the words. He sounded so much like Ezra.

His words had somehow made Joanna relax, but her hands had tightened in her lap at the same time. Maybe she just didn't like the confrontation. She never had, but it seemed like it was more than that,

73

although he couldn't put his finger on it. Maybe the idea that he said he was willing to go out with Whitney instead of 'wanted to' and had ruffled her feathers. He could just about hear the lecture that she would give him about how women wanted to be special and treated like such, and he felt like he had done a pretty good job of salvaging the situation, but maybe that hadn't made her happy. If not, he was sure he would hear about it at some point.

Although not tonight, since he was going home to her rental and she was staying here. Maybe he could talk to her later.

"I'm sorry, Joanna. I will go out of my way to be kind to you." His mother acted like the words had to be pulled from her throat, but they were the right words, and she did nod her head in Joanna's direction.

"I think we both love your son very much and want the absolute best for him. And I think both of us are in agreement that Whitney is beautiful and kind and compassionate, and she and Stonewall might very well be perfect for each other."

Those words made his mother's eyes widen. Then they narrowed with suspicion before that seemed to mostly melt off her face.

"If that's the way you think, then we are, indeed, in agreement." She looked around and then picked up the mashed potatoes. "I do believe we are ready to eat."

Whitney had set everything else on the table and stood beside Dixie as Dixie set the potatoes down.

"You can sit there," Dixie said as she pointed to the chair opposite Stonewall. She herself took the end of the table between Stonewall and Whitney, leaving Joanna kind of hanging out by herself beside Stonewall with two empty spaces in front of her and at the end.

Chapter Eleven

Joanna half expected Stonewall to get up and move to the end, but he did not. Which made her grateful, because she didn't want another scene.

Stonewall said grace, and then as they passed food, Stonewall spoke.

"Joanna and I talked about it and decided that it wouldn't look good for the two of us to stay in her rental together. So we decided that Joanna is going to stay here while I stay there."

Joanna held her breath. That wasn't the way she would have opened the conversation at the table, but she figured Stonewall wanted to get that out of the way if he could.

His mother had the exact reaction that everyone expected

"What?" She paused with the potato scoop in her hand, her eyes big and blinking at Stonewall. "You want her to stay here?" she asked, emphasizing the "her" and the "here."

"I told you. We can't stay at the rental together."

"You can stay here. Let her stay there!"

"Both of us were going to stay at the rental. I had no intention of staying here. It was Joanna and Ezra that said that it probably wouldn't be appropriate for the two of us to stay together. If I'm going to be dating Whitney—" Joanna could only imagine that that sentence was a concession to his mother to try to appease her, but she couldn't know for sure of course. But knowing Stonewall the way she did, she would imagine it to be so. "—it would not be appropriate for me to be here. And it certainly is not appropriate for me to be at the rental with Joanna. That wouldn't be fair to Whitney if we were dating, correct?" he asked, glancing at Whitney for confirmation. Like the poor girl could do anything but nod, which she did.

His mother looked like she wanted to argue, but the way Stonewall had presented it, there really wasn't an argument. If she wanted things to be done properly, and she didn't want Stonewall staying with Joanna, this was the best and only solution.

"That would be fine. Joanna is...can stay here."

Joanna almost laughed. It was obvious that Dixie couldn't quite bring herself to say that Joanna was welcome. But it didn't matter. She'd already known that Dixie didn't really care for her, and while she wasn't exactly sure why, she figured that Dixie had reasons that made sense to her. Wasn't that the way everyone was? Everyone had things that they just couldn't quite overcome and reasons that made sense to them.

Despite the fact that the reasons were also almost always lies, they were lies that the person couldn't see through.

She appreciated Stonewall's defense of her, and she hated to see him arguing with his mother. He saw her so little. Joanna should have done the better thing and allowed him to go by himself. Of course, he had said that he wasn't going to go without her, so there was that, and maybe she should not take credit that wasn't hers.

"It's been unseasonably warm here. I hope that doesn't mean we're in for a hot, dry summer, but I definitely appreciate the warmth after the coldness of the winter. Did you have a bad winter in North Dakota?" Whitney seemed determined to try to make conversation as natural and easy as possible.

Joanna figured that she could meet her halfway. "I think every winter in North Dakota is bad, but this one did seem especially cold and hard."

"The old-timers said it was one of the worst ones they could remember," Stonewall added, picking up a piece of his mother's fried chicken.

Joanna had to admit that Dixie was an excellent cook and she could learn a lot from her if Dixie would be willing to teach her.

They continued with benign conversation, with Dixie eventually joining in and acting like nothing had happened. She didn't give a whole lot of attention to Joanna, but she wasn't unkind, which Joanna appreciated.

"I can help clean up," Joanna said as Stonewall pushed back from his chair, dinner having been long over and the chocolate cake that Dixie had made for dessert still sitting in the middle of the table, half gone.

"Oh, you don't have to," Dixie said right away.

"I'd like to. I'd appreciate it if you'd allow me to." Joanna stood, getting her plate and Dixie's and Stonewall's and taking them to the sink.

She hadn't eaten at Dixie's place much, but she seemed to remember she kept a container by the sink for the scraps to be scraped in which she set out for the cats of the town to eat.

Sure enough, the container she was looking for was there, and she started scraping the plates.

"You did such an excellent job at supper of not letting Dixie get to you." Whitney came over and whispered in her ear as she set her plate down at the sink for Joanna to scrape.

Joanna looked at Whitney, surprised for a moment and then smiling. "Thanks. She's never liked me, and I'm not sure why." She kept her voice low, figuring that Dixie couldn't hear her, since she could hear the low murmur of Stonewall and Dixie's conversation behind them.

"I don't know either." Whitney lifted her shoulder, the expression on her face saying who could explain such things, and she moved away from Joanna and back to the table.

Whitney seemed like such a nice person, and any unkind thoughts that she had toward Dixie should not color her opinion of Whitney. It would be even better if she could figure out a way to get along with Dixie or to make it so that Dixie couldn't help but like Joanna.

But sometimes, the better a person was, the worse the person who disliked them hated them. They wanted to see weakness. Some kind of chink in the armor, some kind of proof that they were just as wicked and evil as they thought. Or maybe it was just the idea that they wanted to see them brought low, because it was easier to like and appreciate someone who wasn't riding high.

Maybe that was what she needed to figure out. What she could do to make it so that she didn't seem perfect in Dixie's eyes, if that was what the problem was.

She'd have to try to figure something out. But in the meantime, she could enjoy friendship with Whitney.

Chapter Twelve

S tonewall wanted to get Joanna alone before he left, but his mother seemed to be intent on having him and Whitney be inseparable. As soon as the dishes were gathered up, she suggested they play games, and then once they had started, she had asked Joanna if she'd like to go upstairs and help her get the bedroom ready that Joanna would be staying in.

Stonewall didn't believe for one second that his mother didn't have a bedroom ready, but he didn't say anything as his mother led Joanna away, leaving him and Whitney alone together.

There was an awkward silence for a while as he shuffled the cards in his hands and tried to think of how he could start the conversation. It felt like he needed to acknowledge his mother's role in all of this somehow and maybe feel her out a bit, trying to figure out if she was a willing pawn, or if there was something else going on.

"I'm sorry about your mother," Whitney said, giving him a perfect opening into the conversation. It made his eyes move to hers as he tried to figure out exactly what she was apologizing for. It seemed like there was a vast array of things he could choose from. From the way she had treated Joanna to the way she had been trying to shove Whitney and him together.

"So you're not part of her conspiracy?" he asked, lacing his words with humor and a smile but really wanting to know.

"The conspiracy to shove Joanna out of your life? Or the conspiracy to insert me into it?"

"Both." That was exactly what he wanted to know.

"I'm definitely not a conspirator to get Joanna out of your life. You two have been best friends since I can remember, and I think everyone in their lifetime should have a best friend like that."

"I agree. She's been a great friend. I only hope I've been half the friend to her that she has been to me."

"I'm sure you have. Don't sell yourself short."

"You don't know how selfish and stupid I can be at times," he said, remembering times when he'd been exactly that and Joanna had overlooked it or maybe not even noticed. Everyone really should have a friend like her. He didn't know why he hadn't seen that before and why he hadn't seen that she would be perfect as a wife as well. She wasn't hard to look at, and while he had never noticed an attraction between them, he could feel it humming through his veins now.

"I'm sure you overestimate that a lot."

He didn't say anything, but then he realized she'd only answered half the question. "And the other conspiracy?"

Her cheeks pinkened, and he had to admit she did look cute with her pink cheeks and her downcast eyes and her hair that fell and partially veiled her face.

"I might be a little bit involved in that one. I mean, I'm not trying to force you into anything, so maybe I should say I'm a willing participant. You are quite a catch, Stonewall. And... There isn't anything going on between you and Joanna, correct? You guys always insisted that you were just friends."

"Yeah. We're just friends." He tried to make his voice sound neutral and not impart the sadness into it that he felt over that. He wanted to be more than friends, but he couldn't say that to Whitney when he hadn't admitted it to Joanna. Joanna was always the first person he told everything to. He wasn't going to allow someone else to usurp her position in his life now. Especially someone that he had just met.

Except, if Whitney was going to be a romantic interest to him, eventually he would have to start telling her things first. Of course.

But they were far from that, and he must have been successful, because her smile grew bigger.

"That's what I thought. Your mom is always so concerned about the two of you. She was sure that you two were going to get married and ride off into the sunset. That you were bewitched by her, and that she led you around on a merry chase, because she had no interest in you and you were just absolutely infatuated with her, and I think that might be part of the reason why your mother finds it so difficult to be nice to her. She thinks that Joanna doesn't appreciate you the way you should be appreciated. And I suppose, if she has no romantic interest in you, I would have to agree with that."

Stonewall swallowed. That had been a pretty speech. And it definitely made Whitney look good. After all, she didn't say a bad thing about Joanna, except for possibly a little bit of gentle criticism because Joanna didn't have any romantic interest in Stonewall, which Stonewall had just admitted was true. So he could hardly say that wasn't true. Because it was.

"I guess my mom is already planning for us to go out, but maybe I should make it official by asking you. Would you go out with me?" It wasn't hard to say. Whitney was a nice girl, but she wasn't the girl he wanted to be asking. She wasn't the girl he wanted to be spending time with, and maybe he was doing them both a disservice.

But maybe not, since he knew that Joanna wasn't the slightest bit interested in him. And maybe he had been looking like a fool all these years, because maybe subconsciously he had been interested in her, and she hadn't been the slightest bit interested in him. Maybe more than one person had noticed that and pitied him because he was so enraptured with her.

That wasn't true. He had voluntarily followed her, and they had talked about what they wanted to do. She had not led him on a merry chase. She'd been beside him all the way, and they'd been friends. Yes. He was sure of that. Whitney seemed to be painting a different picture, but it wasn't an accurate one.

"I would love to. Any day suits me," Whitney said, almost as though she were saying she would clear her calendar for him, and only him. And he would be the most important thing in her life. It did a lot for his ego, except Joanna was like that too. He was the most important thing in her life, there was never any doubt of that. And she was the most important thing in his. Except...if he solidified this date, he would be opening the door for that to change.

"Alright. Tomorrow is Sunday. Would you like to go to church with me?"

Was that disappointment on her face? It was there and gone so fast he could hardly tell. But her smile grew, and she said, "Yes. I'd love that."

He assumed that she meant what she said. She sounded sincere. But that little shadow of disappointment made him say, "Maybe we can go out for lunch afterward, just the two of us."

"That sounds heavenly," she said, and this time, he had no doubt that her answer was sincere and there was not a shred of disappointment on her face. Her hand reached out and covered his. He worked to not pull his hand away. "Please don't let what your mother is trying to force you to do color your actual feelings. Maybe you don't feel anything for me, or maybe you just need to get to know me better. But I know how off-putting it can be when someone pushes you into something. I felt that way before when your mom was pushing us together. But after a few years of looking around and seeing that there really aren't a lot of truly good men who have character and integrity and who do right, and strive to be right, and love Jesus, I guess I realized that I was resisting when I shouldn't have been."

"I guess I wasn't interested then." He wasn't sure he was interested now. "Sometimes timing is everything."

"I cannot disagree with that."

They smiled, and then he used the excuse of shuffling the cards to pull his hand away before he started to deal. Whitney was not a bad person, and he did like her, but...she just didn't seem to hold a candle to Joanna, no matter which way he tried to look at her. Maybe tomorrow it would be different.

Chapter Thirteen

Whitney smiled at Stonewall and tried to make herself feel what she knew she should feel for the handsome man who sat beside her, smiling at her and giving her attention.

Stonewall was a great guy, and she'd always admired him. She definitely considered him handsome and did value his integrity and character just like she told him, but he wasn't the man that her heart had always longed for.

That man had long since gone and hadn't given her a backward glance. She did want to get married and have children, and Stonewall was a great guy. Joanna liked him, maybe even loved him, but that was a friend feeling only, and Whitney felt like Joanna would give her her blessing if Stonewall were to fall in love with her.

Dixie somehow had latched onto her, and Whitney had allowed it. She was successful professionally, but personally her life was lonely.

"Joanna pleaded tiredness, and she's staying upstairs. You two can play as long as you like to. I just came down to grab a drink and let you know that I was retiring for the night," Dixie said as she walked out from the hall into the kitchen.

Stonewall blinked and seemed to be concerned. "Joanna said she wanted to stay upstairs?" he asked, sounding like he couldn't believe it.

"You two have had a very tiring, stressful day. I don't blame her at all, and you shouldn't either." His mother waved her hand, like it was nothing for someone to be tired after such a long trip. Which was true. But Stonewall seemed concerned like it was out of character for Joanna or something else.

He jerked his head and looked back at their card game.

He seemed to have trouble concentrating, and Whitney understood. He was upset that his mother had been so rude to his best friend. Of course, any woman who was going to marry him was not going to want him to be more concerned about his friend than he was about his wife, but they were far from that stage, if they ever got to it.

But he had asked her out.

She did admire him.

"Good night, son. It's good to have you back," Dixie said as she came over and put an arm around her son, giving him a side squeeze and kissing his cheek.

He put an arm around her and squeezed her back, standing to his feet so he could give her a proper hug.

Whitney watched, admiring. She had always loved a man who would put his family first and who would give honor and respect to his mother. Stonewall was certainly that kind of man.

Of course, the man that she lost her heart to all those years ago had been that kind of man too.

She just hadn't been the right person for him, and she needed to accept that and be okay with it.

"Good night, Whitney. Thanks so much for your help with supper tonight. I hope to see you tomorrow at church."

"You will. Stonewall and I are going together, and then we're going out to eat afterward."

"Oh," Dixie said, looking very, very pleased. "I'm thrilled to hear that."

"Should I make sure Joanna comes with us, or are you going to provide something for her to eat?"

"Doesn't she cook?" Dixie asked, and Stonewall's lips flattened. Whitney thought maybe Miss Dixie was going a little bit too far. But

Stonewall shook his head. "She cooks, but this is not her house nor her kitchen, and you wouldn't feel comfortable coming in and taking over someone else's kitchen either."

"I'll make sure she has something to eat. No one in this house will starve while I'm in charge of it," his mother said, and that made his face relax. Whitney only hoped that Dixie was being truthful. She had seen how unkind Dixie could be to Joanna, and Joanna, while she didn't exactly lie down and take it, was too kind to be unkind to Miss Dixie. And now, if the only vehicle they had was Stonewall's, and Stonewall was driving Whitney around, Joanna would have no recourse but to be at home unless Miss Dixie took care of her.

Whitney wouldn't want to be in that situation.

After Dixie had gone to bed, they played in silence for a while.

"So Mom said you have a master's in education. You're still teaching?"

"I am. But I'm hoping that perhaps a principal's job might be mine at some point. If not here, then somewhere. I...I'd like some area of my life to be a success."

"You look like you're successful in a lot of areas," Stonewall said, and she supposed it was a compliment, although he wasn't specific. It was just a general compliment he could have given to a stranger on the street.

"Well, I suppose people would say I'm successful at certain things, but it feels like my personal life needs a facelift. I am lonely at times." Maybe she was saying too much, or maybe he would take that as a broad hint and she didn't really mean it that way, although she supposed if he took it that way, she wouldn't mind.

"I'm sorry about that. I don't know a whole lot about loneliness, considering the size of my family. Sometimes I wish I could be lonely." He laughed a little, and she smiled along with him. She'd always been jealous of his big family. She had been an only child, a child of her parents' later years, and they had both passed away in the last five years. Leaving her alone and lonely.

They finished that card game, with Stonewall chatting about the ranch in Sweet Water and some of the things he did. Every other sentence contained something about Joanna, and Whitney wanted to tell him that if he were looking to find a girl, he was going to have to stop talking about Joanna. It was not exactly a total turnoff, but close.

"If you don't mind, I'm tired. I've driven all day too." Stonewall pushed back away from the table, his eyes raised, as though if she said no, she wanted to continue playing, he would accommodate her. Would he? He probably would. He was that kind of man, but what would that say about her character if she said that she didn't want him to go after he said he wanted to?

"Thank you for playing with me for a bit. And you definitely made your mother happy by coming here to eat. I'll do what I can to make Joanna's life easier." She really would. She didn't want to see anyone suffer, and she really felt like Dixie was a good person, and Joanna definitely did not deserve the way that she had been treated.

"I appreciate that. It feels good to know that Joanna might have an ally. Sometimes my mom can be...a bit like Dracula."

Whitney laughed. "But she's a good lady. And her heart is right. She just wants the best for you. And I'm not sure that she thinks that Joanna has been best for you all these years."

"Joanna has been best for me. I could assure her that, but I don't think it would mean anything." Stonewall's tone was thoughtful, and she didn't figure that he was thinking about what he said, because if he was looking at her as a potential romantic interest, he wouldn't be complimenting Joanna like that. It was on the tip of her tongue to ask if maybe he did indeed have a romantic interest in Joanna, but he said, "I'm looking forward to seeing you tomorrow. Would you like me to pick the restaurant for lunch, or would you like to?"

"You pick it. Surprise me."

She thought maybe he was a little disappointed. Maybe he had no idea what she liked and didn't want to choose something that would upset her. Or maybe he wanted her to take the burden of choosing the restaurant off his shoulders. Then she would have the same problem. What if she picked one he didn't like?

They really didn't know each other at all. And while they had talked about their jobs, they hadn't really gotten to know each other much at all this evening. Maybe tomorrow would be different, but one of them would have to show some interest in order for that to happen, and she could not put all the blame on Stonewall's shoulders, since she was just as guilty. She hadn't shown much interest at all, and in order for her to do that, she was going to have to make a real effort. Shouldn't love be easier?

Chapter Fourteen

I wanted to talk to you before I left.

Joanna looked at her phone. A text from Stonewall had just come in as she sat on her bed after taking a shower and feeling much better now that she and her clothes were both clean. But she'd put her jammies on, and she was ready for bed. Dixie and she had come to a little bit of an understanding she thought as they had made the bed together. Dixie had confessed that she really would like for Stonewall and Whitney to have some time to get to know each other, that she wanted Stonewall to be happy and settled before anything happened to her, and she would like to have grandchildren.

They hadn't exactly declared a truce, but Joanna had assured her that she wanted the same thing for Stonewall, and that she would not stand in the way of Stonewall and Whitney getting together. She had already determined that in her heart anyway, but she didn't say that to Miss Dixie. She didn't even tell Miss Dixie that she had decided that if it was necessary, she would sacrifice and pull back in order for Stonewall to be with the perfect person for him.

I'm already dressed for bed. But I can come down.

Even as she sent the text, she wondered if Miss Dixie was in bed, and if she wasn't, what would she think about Joanna running around the house in her jammies? Would she think that Joanna was breaking her word? She felt like she and Miss Dixie were not exactly friends but had more or less declared a truce. She didn't want to make Miss Dixie feel like she was already not keeping her word.

Please.

Well, that settled it. No matter what Miss Dixie thought, she wasn't going to turn down Stonewall. Since he obviously needed her.

Plus, some people actually went to school or work or shopping in their jammies. Why should she be embarrassed about walking through the house and seeing her best friend in hers?

She threw a sweatshirt on, just because she wasn't sure where he was and in case he wanted to go outside, which would be her preference so there would be less chance of Miss Dixie catching them, and hurried out of her room.

Where are you?

She texted as she hurried down the steps.

Outside on the front porch.

Perfect. She smiled, finding it funny that Stonewall was exactly where she wished he would be. It was uncanny the way they got along like that. It had always been uncanny. But she had always taken it for granted. And sometimes she hadn't even noticed. How foolish she had been to not realize how much they had in common and how unusual that was. Maybe it wasn't even so much that they had a lot in common, but they were just...fit for each other. They weren't even the same in so many areas, but they just...fit.

The downstairs was dark, like everyone else had gone to bed, as she tiptoed through the living room and opened the door, slipping out.

She closed it softly behind her, making out Stonewall's figure in the far corner of the porch, leaning against the post with his arms crossed over his chest and one foot crossed over the other. A casual pose that screamed manly strength and confidence and yet was so familiar to her, since she'd seen him do that a thousand times at their own duplex, as they spent summer evenings together, and even at her family's home, surrounded by brothers in her boisterous family, where Stonewall fit in perfectly and yet never seemed to be consumed by her family, which was saying something, since her family could be rather all-encompassing.

"You survived," she said, just thinking to worry that maybe he was calling her down to tell her that he decided that Whitney was truly the one and he wanted to ask her to do everything in her power to help them get together.

What in the world was she going to do if that was what he wanted?

Well, she was going to help him, of course. That's what friends were for.

"I guess I should say that to you. Considering how ignorant my mother was to you."

"She just loves you. I think we called a truce of sorts upstairs. Did she say anything when she came down?"

"Not really. She made me feel like she had forced you to stay upstairs."

"She did strongly recommend it. But we figured out that we wanted the same thing."

"What's that?" he asked, seeming truly unsure.

"Your happiness." She spoke like it was obvious. Wasn't it? She was his friend. Of course she wanted him to be happy.

"All right. I guess I can buy that, but...how did you staying upstairs manage to secure my happiness? Don't you know I like to be with you? I mean, people have said we're completely inseparable, and I find that to be true. I still don't like to be separated from you. Not that I can't be."

She knew he was speaking the truth. They could be separated. But her family figured out that they worked better when they were paired up. So it was always Joanna and Stonewall together doing something. They just accepted it. And everyone was happier.

"We both want you to be happy, and we both figured that you and Whitney were perfect for each other. Whitney does seem like a nice girl. She's just as sweet as I remember her and accomplished as well. A master's degree. That's impressive."

"I guess. If that kind of thing appeals to you."

"It does to a lot of people." That was the truth. A lot of people put a lot of stock into the degrees that they had and the colleges they went to like it was something very important. And she supposed in certain circles, like educational ones, it was. But it wasn't where she came from. It didn't matter how much book learning a person had if, when they got out of school, they didn't have enough practical knowledge to make anything work. Sometimes it happened. In fact, it happened quite a lot that a person who went to college came back seemingly less intelligent than when they left.

"It's never appealed to me, and you know it."

"I know," she said softly, wondering at the slight belligerence in his tone. "But you have to admit that Whitney is very nice."

"She is. I like her. I asked her out tomorrow."

"On Sunday?" Joanna asked, surprised.

"I asked her to go to church with me. She...seemed a little disappointed about that."

"I can imagine," Joanna said with a small laugh. "I sure hope you're doing something other than just church."

"I'm taking her to lunch too. My mom said that she would make sure you don't starve."

"I can cook, but I hate to take over her kitchen."

"That's what I told her. She seemed to understand. But if you guys have worked things out, then maybe you really will be okay. I didn't want to leave without that reassurance from you. I might not get a chance to talk to you tomorrow. They seem to converge on me, and I feel a little suffocated. And now that I know that you're involved in this plot to push Whitney and I together, I am feeling a little bit like I need air."

"Take all the air you need. I'm not going to push you into

91

something you don't want, but I'm not going to stand in your way. And that's what I told your mom. I want you to be happy, but I didn't want to shove something down your throat. You're welcome to Whitney, I think she's a good girl, but it has to be something that you and Whitney decide together."

"Thank you. You are...amazing. Have I ever told you that?"

"You didn't have to. I just knew you knew it," she said airily with a toss of her head, trying to pawn it off as a joke. Because he sounded way too serious. It made her uncomfortable. After all, she was already thinking that maybe she was wrong about her feelings for him and she had been feeling like he was more than a friend for a long time. This could make it even worse.

"I'm being serious. You're an amazing person. Really special. I... I don't know anyone else like you."

"I feel the same way about you. Now, if you don't mind, it's cold out and I better get back to bed. If your mom comes out here and sees me out in my jammies, she's going to think I went back on my word. Like I'm trying to seduce you with my baggy jammy pants," she said, grabbing a hold of her pants and shaking them, as though to show that there wasn't anything the slightest bit sexy about them.

"They're cute. I like them."

"They're comfortable. And I like them too," she said, emphasizing the word "comfortable," because that was the point of jammies, wasn't it? Something comfortable that one could sleep in. And so comfortable that one just wanted to live in them. Which was probably why so many people decided to go ahead and wear them everywhere.

"Joanna?"

"Yes?" she asked, her back still toward him, her hand on the doorknob. As far as she knew, he hadn't moved

"Thank you."

She wasn't sure what he was saying thank you for, but he was too serious for her tonight, too contemplative, too...different than his normal, and was making her uncomfortable. Not in a bad way, just uncomfortable like this isn't our normal kind of way, and she already knew her heart was in danger of being broken when this good man fell for another woman. Possibly the woman he was taking out on a date the next day.

"You're welcome," she said, having no idea what he was thanking her for. "Good night." She didn't look behind her but pulled the door open and stepped through it. She heard his soft "good night" as she quietly closed it behind her.

Maybe if her eyes hadn't been used to the dark, she wouldn't have seen the shadowy figure that stood just inside the kitchen doorway.

Dixie had seen her.

Chapter Fifteen

"I'd love it if you could come in for a little bit," Whitney said. They were back from their lunch date after church, and the day hadn't been terrible. Joanna had sat with his mother during church, and Whitney and Stonewall had sat on the other side of her. His mother hadn't been obvious about it, but somehow she had inserted herself between Stonewall and Joanna and he hadn't gotten a chance to talk to her all day. Of course, since he had asked Whitney for a date and offered to take her to church, he shouldn't have been trying to sit beside Joanna.

But he had tried to talk to her last night, and she had been dismissive. She hadn't wanted to hear the seriousness in his tone. Normally she was very sensitive to any change in his tone or to the things that he might not be saying. She might wait for him to come around, to decide to talk to her about whatever it was he was thinking, but she knew that there was something. Last night, she had deliberately ignored it.

Of course, he didn't know that. But he was just judging from the way she had acted before. It seemed like a good deduction, since it was outside of the norm.

And there he was thinking about Joanna again.

"No thank you. I suppose I would like to go home and take a rest."

It wasn't entirely true. He wanted to go to his mom's and see Joanna. But his mom had texted that she and Joanna were taking a Sunday afternoon nap. Maybe that text was to let him know that he didn't need to bother to come because Joanna wasn't going to be available. It seemed the only reason he could think of for his mom to send a text like that.

"All right. I hope I'll see you again."

"I'm sure you will. I suppose you're back to work tomorrow."

"Yes. Teachers work Monday through Friday. But I do have the weekends off. And do you want to do something next weekend?" Whitney asked, her head tilted coyly, her expression inviting. He had gotten the feeling that she really did like him. And to be honest, he liked her too. But he just didn't feel anything for her, if that made sense.

Nothing like the deep emotions that ran through him when he thought about Joanna. He wanted to protect her, to be with her, to just sit with her in silence. He didn't even need to talk to her in order to be satisfied. It was just the idea of her being near. He didn't feel anything like that with Whitney. Maybe that was just because he didn't know her as well.

"Are you free Friday night?" he asked, wondering if maybe he would regret that. But he had promised three dates.

"I am!" Whitney said, a huge smile breaking over her face. "Would you like to do something?" she added, and he tried not to be annoyed. He was going to ask her out, and she flipped the tables and asked him.

He supposed that was better than being turned down, but he wanted to be the one who controlled the narrative. Not her.

Since when did that happen? He and Joanna just did it naturally. Whenever their strengths came up, that's whoever was in charge. And they did it without talking or fussing or even discussing it.

Again, that was probably just because they had spent so much time together. If he and Whitney were going to be together, they would figure it out eventually.

And he needed to think about that, since Joanna had seemed distinctly disinterested last night.

He did not kiss her goodbye but waved a hand, thanking her for a

95

pleasant morning and meal, and stepped back off the porch, feeling like he had been freed from something.

It wasn't supposed to feel that way, was it? It wasn't supposed to feel like he was relieved to get away from her, if she was the one he was supposed to spend the rest of his life with. How was he going to get away from her if that's what was going to happen?

He thought about swinging by his mother's house, just to see if Joanna was up, but he didn't, instead driving straight to the Clybourns' rental. He considered it his as well. The Clybourns' money had supported him since before he had graduated from high school, but that was because he was with Joanna all of that time. They had done everything together.

Maybe he needed to think about being by himself. Although, just because he and Joanna weren't together anymore, just because he might find someone new, didn't mean that he couldn't continue to work for the Clybourns, did it?

That was a good question, considering that everything that he had done for the Clybourns had been beside Joanna. Knowing the Clybourns the way he did, they would never tell him that he would have to go somewhere else to work if he was no longer Joanna's best friend. They considered him one of the family. They said that often enough. That he and Joanna were family.

But now they weren't.

It kind of felt that way. He felt bereft, lonely, sad as he pulled into the rental and got out by himself.

When was the last time he spent Sunday afternoon alone?

Joanna had gone shopping with some of her sisters for Christmas. He had stayed with the men and continued to work on the farm. But she'd only been gone one afternoon, and they'd been texting the whole time. She had taken pictures of the things she wanted to buy and asked what he thought. He had asked her to go ahead and pick up some things for him, and she had obliged. Shopping wasn't something either one of them enjoyed, but she did it for him because he'd asked.

He smiled a little at the memory. She'd not been with him, but it felt like she had. That made sense. Now, it didn't feel like she was with him at all.

Why didn't he text her?

He made it into the kitchen and got a glass of water from the tap, drinking half of it before he set it down on the counter and pulled his phone out of his pocket.

> Are you up?

He sent the text and decided that maybe he would go lie down on his bed for a little bit. He had a lot of work to do, and he grabbed a notebook and a pen from the drawer and figured he'd take it up with him, writing down the things that he knew that he was going to need to buy. He'd noticed that the hardware store in town was closed and wasn't the slightest bit surprised since it was Sunday. Small town stores often were closed on Sundays.

> Yeah. Your mom wanted me to take a Sunday afternoon nap, insisted on it actually. So, I'm in my room. Bored out of my mind, but she saw me come in last night from talking to you, and I figured I'd better stay put.

> She saw you?

He hadn't realized. Man, maybe he had jeopardized the tenuous relationship Joanna had tried to form with his mother by asking her to come down and possibly getting her into trouble. He knew when he said please she would not refuse him.

> Yeah. She was standing in the kitchen doorway when I came in. She didn't say anything, and I pretended I didn't see her because what was I going to say? But if she saw me go out, she knew I was not there long.

> Thankfully. I'm sorry. I didn't realize I might get you in trouble.

It's not you. But I've been trying to be good and careful so that she realizes that we want the same thing.

My happiness. I know.

Joanna didn't send anything after that. And he sat there with his phone, finally laying it on his chest. He was more convinced than ever after spending the morning with Whitney that Whitney was not going to make him happy.

First of all, he believed happiness was a choice, but Whitney wasn't what he wanted.

What he wanted was a woman that he couldn't have. Apparently. Since she was his best friend, and that's all she saw him as.

He determined that he wasn't going to sit and wallow. If she didn't want him, he would try as hard as he could to make things work with Whitney. She believed the way he did, she was sweet and kind and was ready to settle down. She was basically everything he was looking for, except she wasn't Joanna, if he had been looking to settle down, which he didn't really think he was. Would it hurt for him to just go back to the ranch and still be best friends with Joanna?

Could he do that knowing that his feelings for her changed?

He honestly wasn't sure.

It wouldn't hurt to try to make things work with Whitney for a few weeks, and he resolved to do just that.

Chapter Sixteen

After lying in his bed and writing a list of the things that he needed, Stonewall decided to get up and start working on the house. He lost track of time, and before he knew it, the sun had gone down, and darkness had settled over.

He was hungry and hadn't gone grocery shopping or even thought about food.

If Joanna was there, one of them would have said that they were hungry, and one of them would have bounced off the idea that maybe they should go pick up some food so they didn't starve to death. But he'd been so sunk in his thoughts that he hadn't even thought about food until he needed it.

He realized that there were noises coming from outside, and he set the hammer he'd been using down and walked to the window.

The kids that had been using this as their hangout must be back. He saw some bodies moving around the side yard and heard a few people talking, and now that he was thinking about it, he heard music as well.

They must have ignored his truck sitting in the front or assumed that he was parked there but visiting someone else.

He saw a couple together, a teenage boy, all lanky arms and legs with a beanie cap pulled down low over his head and his pants loose around his hips, in what seemed to be the popular punk style. He had his arm around a girl. She wore a tank top and jeans that looked like they'd been painted on. She had to be cold if the kid needed a hat to keep warm. But maybe the alcohol she held in her hand was keeping her warm so she didn't realize she was freezing.

But it wasn't the alcohol, which was surely illegal, that caught his attention. It was the way they moved together. He had one hand around her, one hand on his beer, his head down, nuzzling her neck, as their bodies moved together to the music.

It was obvious what the boy wanted, and it was obvious that the girl wanted the same thing or was at least doing a great job of pretending.

He stood and watched for a bit, knowing that he needed to go out and do something, since it was completely illegal for the minors to be drinking at the very least and who knew what else was going on there.

But for a while, he just stood and watched, knowing that that could have been him. Very easily could've been him. His mom had tried to raise him right, but if he had not had Joanna and the Clybourn family, he was pretty sure he would have been taken in by a group like this. Instead, he'd been taken in by a group of upright homeschoolers, who had treated him like part of the family, put him to work, and expected him to earn his keep while treating him like they loved and respected and trusted him. It had been unlike anything he had ever known, and it all started when Joanna had seen him hanging around town by himself, dressed very much like that young kid outside his window was dressed now.

Maybe he'd been a few years younger, slightly less rebellious, and definitely a lot more lonely, because he hadn't had a girl to snuggle up with. But he and Joanna had hit it off to the point where he hadn't needed one. Hadn't been interested. And the Clybourns had treated him like he was upright and righteous, and he had wanted to be that way. Eventually he had found his own relationship with Jesus, and the teachings he had learned in the church with his mom had made sense.

Thankfully he hadn't gone so far down the rebellious road he couldn't get back, and he had spent every spare second he could with Joanna and her family.

He even spent his senior year being homeschooled by Caleb and Phoebe who had tag teamed him and the younger siblings.

He'd only needed one English class to graduate, and he had done better in that English class and learned more than he had in his entire years in school. He assumed it was the company.

The couple was kissing now, the boy's hand holding the beer draped over the girl's shoulder, his hips moving suggestively and the girl pressing closer.

He could have really screwed up his life. Screwed it up to the point where the idea of having a girl like Whitney, successful and educated and confident, would've been way out of his reach. He probably would have been in jail.

He had Joanna to thank.

Joanna and the whole Clybourn family.

With that thought, knowing he had no weapon with which to protect himself in case this gang was a lot more unruly than what he thought it was, he stepped away from the window, walked to the door, and stepped outside.

He startled two kids who were making out on the porch.

"Nice evening," he said casually as the girl straightened her clothes and the boy scrambled to his feet, looking like he was ready to run. At Stonewall's casual words, he stopped and looked back.

"Are you squatting here too?" the kid said, his eyes narrowed, definitely not trusting Stonewall.

"No. I own the place." He didn't exactly own the place, but he figured that was close enough to the truth.

These teens didn't seem like they were going to quibble about details, and he was living here, so it was what it was.

The girl had fixed herself and was still standing behind the boy, completely hidden, not even trying to peek out over his shoulder.

"Aren't you going to kick us out?" the kid asked, still sounding annoyed and rebellious.

"I suppose that's probably what you expect me to do. I don't think there are too many people around town who would want you to make out on their front porch."

"I'm not doing drugs."

"I didn't say you were."

"You just looked like you were going to."

"What's going on over here?" The kid that Stonewall had seen through the window dancing with the girl came around the side, probably made bolder by the alcohol that he had consumed.

"Dude says he lives here," the kid from the porch said, jerking his head at Stonewall who stood there, his arms hanging down, trying to strike a casual pose.

"Nobody lives here. You're trespassing. You better get out before I call the cops," the kid said, and Stonewall had to hand it to him. The kid had some brass and confidence.

"That's scary. If I didn't live here, I would probably be afraid. But since I do, I'm welcoming the cops if they come. I suppose I would like them to figure out who's been littering on my property and make them clean it up."

"We can clean it up if you don't call the cops," the first kid said, and that time, the girl did peek out over his shoulder to get a better view of this adult who didn't act the way she thought he should.

"I guess that sounds like a good compromise. You pick up the trash that you left here on your previous visits, and I won't call the cops to let them know that you're trespassing, littering, and drinking alcohol despite the fact that you're not old enough to."

It was a wild guess but an accurate one since all four of the kids looked extremely guilty.

Again, Stonewall had the distinct feeling that this could totally be him. And for some reason, it made him feel sad, almost sad to his soul. Sad that these kids didn't have a family like the Clybourns who could take them in and change their life. Didn't have a friend like Joanna who could love him for who he was, who would see him on the street and see the potential there, could bring him home and make him feel valued and needed and help him grow into a man that had character and integrity and was able to make his own way in life.

Maybe he wasn't going to spend the rest of his life with Joanna, but maybe he could pass a little of what she did for him on.

Chapter Seventeen

"Thank you for supper, it was delicious." Joanna set the last plate in the dishwasher and closed the door.

"I don't want you to thank me. You're the one who made it," Miss Dixie said, her face actually softening into a bit of a smile. She hadn't said anything about seeing Joanna coming in from outside the night before, but Joanna had been very careful to be on her extremely best behavior, and Miss Dixie had been content, even kind, the longer the day went on and Joanna stayed with her rather than looking up Stonewall.

She kind of expected Stonewall to show up, but he didn't. She had to admit, it had been a hard, lonely day for her. It had been a long time since she and Stonewall had not been together, and there was part of her that felt like, while it was hard and sad, it was probably a good thing, something for her to get used to, since Stonewall might even now still be with Whitney and perhaps making the decision that Whitney was someone he could spend the rest of his life with.

She wanted to know how their date went, wanted to know what was said, wanted to know how he was feeling and what he thought. But he hadn't texted again, and neither had she. She truly didn't want to interrupt their date or their time together, if they were getting to know each other and if Whitney and he could fall in love. At least, she told herself she didn't. Even while she wished that she could do something to make him fall in love with her. Because the idea of him with Whitney was tearing her up. She didn't want him to be with Whitney. She wanted him to be with her.

There. She admitted it to herself.

"If you don't mind, I'm going to take a little walk. Would you like to come with me?" she asked as she looked around at the spotlessly clean kitchen.

"You go on ahead. I think I'm going to sit down and read a book for a while."

"All right. I won't be out long. And you can text me if you need me." She had given Miss Dixie her phone number while they ate lunch after church. They'd had a nice chat, and Miss Dixie had been nice, if not extremely kind. She supposed she still had reservations, but the fact that Joanna was not trying to do anything to get between Whitney and Stonewall seemed to allay some of her fears. Perhaps that really had been the only thing that Miss Dixie had held against Joanna. Although, back when they were younger, she had been upset that Joanna had seemed to monopolize all of Stonewall's time. Maybe she had just wanted to spend time with her son. But to hear the way Stonewall told it, she hadn't been a very interested mother.

Maybe he just felt like that because teenagers often did. She didn't know.

Still, she grabbed a jacket and stepped outside into the cool evening air. It was only a few blocks to the rental where Stonewall was staying, and despite herself, her feet turned in that direction. She tried to tell herself that she needed to know what they needed to get tomorrow so they could start working on it. Because Whitney and Miss Dixie weren't the whole reason they were there. Both of them were expecting to spend time working when Stonewall wasn't with his mom. And if he had made any plans to be with her during the week, Joanna didn't know about them.

She felt like she had been away from him for a month instead of the day, like she had missed so much and she wanted to catch up on it all.

Maybe that's why her feet took her in the direction that she knew she shouldn't go. She should at least take off in the other direction so that she could reassure Miss Dixie and have her see that she wasn't going straight to Stonewall, but she couldn't even manage to take that much of a detour just to reassure the older woman.

Fifteen minutes later, she stood in front of the rental, blinking.

There were lights on everywhere and people coming and going. All the trash had been cleaned up, and a young kid, maybe fifteen or sixteen, was kneeling on the porch while Stonewall showed him how to measure the gap in order to cut a board for it.

Joanna shoved her hands in her pockets and just watched while Stonewall worked with the kid. He obviously found the key to the shed in one of the drawers and had gotten the tools out. But that wasn't what amazed her.

It was the fact that the kids who had been hanging out, throwing all the garbage around, were now hanging out, picking up the garbage, and helping to clean up the house, and it was all Stonewall's doing.

If she had been here, surely she would have suggested that they shoo everyone away. She didn't want a bunch of ragamuffins hanging around, potentially hurting people, and disrupting the peace. Not to mention all the empty beer cans lying around, and this kid was not old enough to be drinking.

She had to admit, she was kind of impressed with what Stonewall had done with his time without her. Had she been holding him back all this time? Although, she also had to admit that she was relieved that he wasn't still with Whitney.

Thinking of the woman made Joanna look around. She couldn't see her anywhere, but that didn't mean that she wasn't working with someone in the house. Maybe she was still here.

And that made Joanna feel worse. There she was, having been with Stonewall for years and years, and he'd never done anything like this, and just one day with Whitney, and she had him rehabilitating the neighborhood. Whitney was definitely better for him than Joanna was.

With that thought, Joanna turned and was going to walk away. But Stonewall must have looked up just at that time and seen her.

"Joanna?" he said, as though he couldn't believe it was her. Had it just been a day? Because they could recognize each other even in the dark. At least they'd been able to before now.

"Yeah?" she said, turning around.

"What are you doing? Why are you walking away?"

"Sorry. You just looked busy."

She didn't bother to say the things she'd been thinking. She knew that sometimes her mind had a tendency to chew on things that couldn't possibly be true or to get hooked on things that she didn't know were true.

"Stay. You can meet Declan and Tyler and Taylor and Sharee. They've been helping me clean up."

"I can see. Looks really good." The sun had dropped below the horizon a while ago, the air had cooled down, and the light was fading, but it was obvious that the house looked a lot better than it had when they had gotten there yesterday.

"You have to see the interior, but let me introduce you to these guys. They're pretty good workers."

Joanna smiled, feeling awkward with Stonewall, which was so unusual that it made her feel even worse than she already did.

He introduced her to the kids, who claimed that they needed to go. The smell of alcohol permeated the air, but the kids were respectful, and some of them even said that they might show up after school the next day.

At least twenty minutes went by before Stonewall said, "Can you come in for a little bit?"

"I can't stay too long. Your mom will wonder where I am. And... I know I should have taken off in the exact opposite direction, but my feet took me here. I missed you today."

She did not mean to say that. Did not. But the words were out, and they seemed to make him happy, because he smiled, looking back at her as he opened the door before stepping back and allowing her to walk in first.

"That's good to hear. Because I really missed you too."

"It doesn't look like it. You have all kinds of friends hanging around here. Where's Whitney?" There, she ended that statement with the question that she really didn't want to ask either. Well, she wanted to ask it, but she didn't want to ask it of him.

"Whitney?" His brows furrowed like he didn't even know her. Who was this person?

"You and Whitney were together this morning. You went to church, and you were going out? I assume she came back to your place, or you went to hers?"

"Good night, no." He sighed heavily while putting an arm around her shoulder, in a buddy type caress, one that they had done a million times, and guided her to the kitchen. "I don't know why I'm bringing you to the kitchen. There's nothing here. But I'm starving."

She laughed. "I didn't think about getting groceries either, but your mom had food, so I've had supper." She lifted her shoulder. "Sorry."

"No, that's fine. I guess I blamed you that I didn't have food, because if you'd been here, you'd have been complaining that you were hungry, and one of us would've figured out that we didn't have any food in the house and we needed to go get some."

"Wow. I leave the guy for a day, and he almost starves to death."

"That's not the half of it," he said, and she wondered what he meant. She also wanted to go back to the subject of Whitney. He seemed...relieved that he hadn't been with her. That wasn't exactly what his mother wanted, and while it wasn't exactly what she wanted either, there was a part of her that was hoping and praying it was true, because she was going to feel lighter.

"Do you mind if we go get something?" he asked. "I promise I'll be quick."

She really wanted to, but there was a part of her that didn't want to upset his mother.

"It has to be fast," she said, raising her brows.

"It will be. I'll stop at the closest gas station that's open, get a hot dog, and that'll tide me over until tomorrow when we go grocery shopping."

He said "we," and it made her insides smile and jump up and down. She was still a part of him, even though he'd spent time with Whitney.

He laughed. "I know I just led you into the kitchen, but come on, let's head out to the truck."

"All right. Just lead me on a merry chase."

He put his arm around her shoulder again, hooking it over the top, like she was his buddy again. She did not mind. She relished the weight of his arm on her, his heat beside her, his presence, his laughter, everything she missed today and worried that she would never get to experience again, even though she knew it wasn't true. But everything she worried she was losing.

He opened the door to the house and then the pickup like he'd been doing the last few times they'd gotten in. She murmured a thank you and then resolved that if he didn't start talking about Whitney, she was going to ask.

Chapter Eighteen

Stonewall could barely contain his happiness at seeing Joanna. He couldn't wait to get rid of all of his new friends, which didn't say a whole lot for his character, but he was relieved when they all said that they were leaving. He hoped to have more supplies and really did hope that they came back the next day, because he was excited about working with them, potentially changing a life the way Joanna changed his, but he wanted to be with Joanna, had missed her more than he could say, and needed just to be with her even for a little bit.

It bothered him some that she wasn't asking about Whitney and making sure that everything was okay there, that he wasn't leaving her, but he reminded himself that she didn't feel the same way about him that she felt about her.

"You sounded relieved that Whitney was gone. Did you guys not have a good time?"

"You're too astute. You always are. You know exactly what I'm thinking. I don't even know why you asked."

She laughed but then said, "So it didn't go well?"

It was not hope in her voice. In fact, he thought it was disappointment and a little bit of compassion like she felt bad for him, like he had somehow given her the idea that he liked Whitney and would be hurt if it didn't go well.

"No. I think it went okay. We have a date for Friday night. She works during the week, of course."

"Of course," Joanna said, and he almost felt like there was forced cheerfulness in her voice. That was odd.

"But I felt relief when I walked away from her after taking her home from lunch. I mean, like I was free. Isn't that weird?"

"I don't know. Maybe you were just nervous, and it was a freedom from your nerves."

"Maybe. I suppose it could have been, but I just felt like finally, I can breathe again. And it wasn't necessarily because I was nervous, I don't think."

"You enjoyed being with her?"

"I guess. Conversation was awkward at times, but I suppose that's what happens when two people are getting to know each other."

"I'm sure it is."

"Yeah, so anyway, we didn't linger over our meals, and she did invite me in. But I don't know if she wanted me to go in any more than I wanted to. I feel like she likes me but not that much. Like she wants to like me more than she actually does."

"Interesting way to feel."

"Maybe that's just because that's the way I feel. I feel like I should like her. She's perfect. But...I'm not sure I do."

"There's nothing wrong with her." Her tone almost made the statement a question.

"Nothing at all." He was quiet for a moment. "But she just doesn't seem to be what I want."

"But she would be someone you could get along with?"

"I suppose." He didn't say anything more, then changed the subject. "What did you and my mom do all day?"

"We came home from church, had lunch, took a nap, got up, chatted for a bit and sat on the front porch, and then went in, and I made some supper. Then I told her I was taking a walk. I...missed you."

"I missed you too." It was a big admission, but he appreciated that she admitted that she missed him as well. "You realize that the last time we were apart was when you went Christmas shopping, and we texted the whole day."

"I didn't really feel like we were apart that day. Because I was doing your shopping for you. I kept sending you pictures, and you kept saying 'yeah, that's fine,' and I was like, 'I want your opinion, not just to hear it's fine.'"

"I know. You got so mad you called me. So yeah, that was a good day."

"The day I got mad at you?"

"You weren't really mad. You were just frustrated I wasn't helping you more, and you hated shopping, and I was just having fun because I didn't have to shop. And then I felt guilty because you were doing my shopping for me, and I figured that I probably ought to at least put a little bit of effort into it."

"That's right. You shouldn't leave me to do all the dirty work by myself."

"That's just the point. You don't do the dirty work by yourself, and I don't do the dirty work by myself. We do it together. Everything. And today was...not like that."

They were quiet for a little bit as he pulled into the convenience store. He sat with his hands on the wheel and didn't try to get out.

"And I wondered to myself, maybe that's the way it needs to be. Because if I'm not going to marry you, I probably ought to get used to being away from you, unless we're just going to go back to the ranch and pretend everything is the same."

It wasn't what he wanted. But what else could he say?

Chapter Nineteen

"So I started working here, and the kids who were helping me gave me a hand with that as well." Stonewall showed Joanna where he had started working the day before.

They walked around the house, discussing things, but it just didn't feel the same. He wasn't sure quite what the problem was. She seemed to have withdrawn when he suggested that they ought to get used to being away from each other. It hadn't sounded right as it was coming out of his mouth, and while she hadn't had a terrible reaction, she'd gotten quiet, and this morning, she hadn't been back to her old self.

He couldn't blame everything on her. Because he wasn't back to his old self either.

Shouldn't he be thinking about Whitney? Shouldn't he be wondering whether she was going to school and what she was doing or what was going on with her? But instead, his sole focus was Joanna. A normal person wouldn't even have noticed a change in her demeanor or actions, but he was so in tune with her, that was obvious immediately.

Any time before, he would just talk to her about it. That's what friends did. And he wasn't afraid to talk to her about anything, except... He did not want to talk to her about this. If he mentioned what he was really thinking, what he really wanted, which was to see if maybe they could have a romantic relationship, it could end up ruining their relationship past repair. He'd known several people who had been friends and tried dating, and it ruined everything. He'd even known people who had gotten married after being friends for a long time, and now they didn't even talk to each other after their divorce. He didn't want that to be Joanna and him. But if he ended up with someone else, or she did, which gave him an even worse feeling, they would probably be going their separate ways anyway, right? After all, what he said about them getting used to spending time away from each other, since that's the way it would probably be, made as much sense as anything else.

"And so you can see, I don't think there's a whole lot of work to do here."

They had ended up back in the kitchen, where there were a few cupboard doors that needed hinges and that type of thing.

"I made a list of the things that I thought we should pick up at the hardware store today."

She leaned against the sink before she said, "It's probably open now."

"Yeah. I saw the sign yesterday that said it opens at nine, so we can definitely go and get the stuff picked up. You want to take a look at my list and see if you noticed anything else we might need?"

He had the fixtures and equipment that they needed on one side, and he put the boards and stuff that they would need to get from a larger fix-it store in a different column. He held the paper up to her, and she took it from him, glancing over it.

He took the time to study her. Her slender fingers, her serious expression, which broke so easily into a smile. The way she teased him out of his bad moods over the years, and he had done the same for her. The way they could laugh at each other without being offended. The way they could finish each other's sentences but still gave each other the respect of listening. He just never felt more comfortable with anyone. Never felt more like he fit with someone than with her.

He noted that the hand that held the paper had dropped to her side, and she seemed to stare out the window a bit before she turned to him.

"I was really impressed when I saw how you are working with the kids who gathered around. That's just something that is so you, and I'm sorry that I missed it."

"Well, you didn't miss everything. They said they would be back. Whether or not they will, I don't know."

"I bet they will. It seemed like everyone was having a great time, and you're so good at that."

She was sincere. And her compliment made his chest swell. Still, as nice as she was being, it didn't feel the same. There was a reserve about her that hadn't been there before. And he wished he could break through it. But maybe that was her way of pulling away a bit, so the final break wouldn't hurt so much. He could certainly understand that.

"I was wondering how we should spend time with your mom. Or maybe, maybe I guess I was wondering how I should spend time with your mom. I don't want to pry, because I know that what you're doing with Whitney is none of my business, but—"

"What do you mean it's none of your business? You're my best friend. Of course it's your business."

She gave him a look that he interpreted to mean that if he was having a romantic relationship, it really wasn't her business. But she didn't say anything.

"I just know that you're here, and your mom would like to spend some time with you if she can." She paused for a moment. The paper in her hand fluttered as she ran her fingers over it, and then she set it down on the counter, putting her hand on top of it and smoothing it out. "I would like to spend some time with her too. I feel like she and I are growing in our relationship toward each other, and it makes me feel good to think that someone who didn't like me might have changed their minds. But part of that is me staying completely away from you and Whitney anytime you're together."

"Yeah. That does make her happy to think that you are on her team, quote, unquote, in helping to get Whitney and I together." He tried not to sound bitter about that. He didn't want to be together with Whitney. He wanted to be together with Joanna. But Joanna was strong-arming him every which way he turned. She might be even more than strong-arming him, she was pushing him toward Whitney. Encouraging him to be with her and wanting to spend time with his mother.

"I guess maybe I thought I could go home around lunchtime and give her a hand making food, and then we'll see if she wants to bring it out here, or you could come there and eat?"

"Of course. It's not that far, and you're right. I'm here. I should be spending time with my mom."

"I know on the farm sometimes we work until dark or later, but... she might like to spend mealtimes with us and some time in the evening..."

"I kind of figured that the kids from school would be here in the evening. Maybe Mom would be interested in making a meal for everyone around four. I know I was always starved when I got home from school."

"I remember that."

He nodded his head and then said what he had wanted to say earlier. "What you said about the kids that were here and what I did..."

"I know. That was just pretty amazing. Anyone else would have run them out of here."

"No. Not anyone else. You took this stray in when we were just kids." He pointed to himself. And watched Joanna, until she raised her eyes to his, and he saw comprehension dawn.

She shook her head. "You were never drinking beer and doing anything terrible."

"If it hadn't been for the grace of God and how He had our paths cross, and you having mercy on me, then it might have been me. I couldn't help but think that as I was watching them out the window. They didn't realize I was in here at first, and I stood there thinking about how your family had changed the trajectory of my life. And how I had the opportunity to do that yesterday with some people. Maybe not the same as what your family did, but close. And when I say 'your family,' they were part of it, but you're the one that I really am grateful to."

"That was definitely the Lord. As soon as I met you, we just seemed to click. I mean, it was like I met the other part of myself. And I can't remember a time when I didn't want you with me."

She had never said that before, at least not in those words or not in the way it hit him just now. It sounded like something that a girlfriend would say to a boyfriend or a wife to a husband.

"Joanna?"

"Yes?"

They looked at each other for a bit as the words trembled on his tongue. He wanted to ask her if they could be more. If friendship was all they would ever have. If he was crazy for thinking these thoughts about her, and if he should just be content with the friend that he had and the opportunity for an excellent girlfriend in Whitney. But the fear of ruining the relationship won out, and he swallowed those words.

"Thanks. Thanks for being such a great friend all these years."

He didn't think he had ever thanked her. Not for being his friend. It was just something he took for granted. Something he just assumed was going to be there. Her friendship, her companionship, her laughter, and her sunny disposition.

"I should say the same for you. You've been just as good of a friend to me as I have been to you. I mean, it takes a pretty good friend to move across the country to be with someone."

"Wyoming to North Dakota is not across the country, and that was my job. Not that I didn't want to still continue to be with my friend, but I was getting paid by that time, and your family was my family. How could I not go?"

He was downplaying the fact that he would follow Joanna anywhere. Whether her family was paying him or not. But she smiled and nodded.

"So all right, we got the gushy stuff out of the way. Now, we'll see if your mom will make us a list so we can get some groceries for her and if she's willing to cook at four every afternoon, and I'll leave around eleven to give her a hand with lunch, and that takes care of the food part."

"That's the most important part."

They laughed together. And he picked the list up off the counter, accidentally brushing her fingers as he did so. He'd brushed her fingers a million times, touched her without thinking about it, but for some reason, her fingers, cool and soft, made his hand want to linger. It was all he could do to continue to pull the list away.

"So we gonna make a parts run?"

Normally it wouldn't need to be a question. They would have just gone out to the truck and gone together. And done it without thinking. But with the new way their relationship was going, he wasn't sure where they stood.

"How about I stay here, and I can work on a few of the things that can be done with equipment that we have. And you can go ahead and grab everything that we need and bring it back. Then it will be time for me to go give your mom a hand with lunch."

Was that really why she suggested that? Or was it not because she wanted to spend time with his mom, but because she wanted to put a distance between them? Minimize the time they worked together. Get used to being apart?

"I don't know if I can find all of the stuff without you," he murmured, not wanting to say he didn't want to do it without her. He could. Of course. He was a grown man, and he didn't need Joanna to hold his hand everywhere he went. But... He liked it. And if it truly was going to end, he wanted to spend every last second he could with her and cherish it.

"Oh, that's right. I forgot you seem to have the male predisposition to being unable to see things that are right in front of your nose."

"Seems to me that you've done that a time or two."

"You're right. So between the two of us, we ought to be able to find that stuff. All right. I'll go with you."

Chapter Twenty

"This chili smells delicious," Dixie said, coming over to the counter where Joanna stood stirring the pot on the stove.

"It should. You made most of it."

"I would say it was more evenly split between the two of us."

Joanna laughed, loving that Dixie was finally being, if not super sweet to her, at least nice. It felt good.

"Should we take sour cream and cheese and that type of thing?" Miss Dixie asked.

They were having chili for lunch, and Miss Dixie said that she would make mashed potatoes and cornbread to go along with it for when the kids got off school.

"Stonewall hates sour cream, but he'll take all the cheese you'll put on it."

Dixie gave her a look before she nodded and grabbed cheese out of the refrigerator. "Do you like sour cream?"

"I can live without it. I do like it, but there's no need to carry everything in the refrigerator out."

"If you like it, we'll take it. I'm like Stonewall. I like the cheddar and nothing else." She looked at the refrigerator for a moment. "Would he rather have water or tea?"

"He likes tea with as much sugar in it as you can get it to take without clumping on the bottom." Joanna laughed.

"Got it." Dixie closed the refrigerator door, taking the pitcher of tea and setting it on the counter where she took the lid off and added sugar to it. "You really do know Stonewall extremely well."

"I should. We've spent so much time together that I ought to be able to figure out the things that he likes and doesn't like. I'd have to be extremely self-centered to not."

"I take it that means that he knows you just as well?" Miss Dixie said as she stirred the tea, the spoon plinking against the sides of the container.

"Better probably. He's a lot more considerate and thoughtful than I am. He's always inspired me to be better."

"It's nice to be around people who inspire you to be better."

"I agree. My siblings have always said that." In fact, that's what Ezra had always said they should look for in a spouse. It's what he said that their parents always told him. He knew their parents better than she did. Although she had some great memories and remembered some of the things they'd taught, she'd been so young when they died.

Still, Ezra had done his best, along with Phoebe and Priscilla and Caleb and all of the older siblings, to pass down to the younger ones the things that their parents had taught.

One of those things had been that it was wise to choose a spouse who encouraged you and inspired you to be better.

Joanna thought about the kids that Stonewall had been helping on Sunday evening. She probably would have chased those kids away, but he had given her credit for taking him under her wing. Not that she had taken him under her wing exactly, but it had been less of an altruistic type of thing and more of a selfish, I like this kid and we get along together, so I want to spend more time with him kind of thing. Yet Stonewall gave her credit where it wasn't due and said that she was the reason, along with her family, that he felt like he needed to pass it on.

And yet, he was the one who inspired her. With his kindness and consideration and the way he was always trying to do things to be kind and helpful and to make her life easier.

"Do you think the kids will like the chili?" Miss Dixie asked as she put the lid back on the tea and set the spoon she had been using to stir in the sink.

"Yesterday when you asked them, they all claimed to. I think the mashed potatoes are going to be a big hit as well. That garnered an even bigger reaction." They had been feeding the kids every day that week, and they had done really well. Today, Stonewall was going to leave early because of his date with Whitney, and Joanna and Dixie were going to do supper themselves.

"Do you think they'll leave once they're done eating?" Miss Dixie asked, and there seemed to be a little bit of fear in her voice.

"They might. Or we could put them to work again. Although they worked every night this week, and we told them they didn't need to work this evening if they didn't want to."

"I just wonder if they'll feel like they need to hang around or...do violence or something."

"I don't think they'll do that. I could be wrong, but Stonewall told them he would pay them tomorrow, and I think they're pretty excited about getting paid for the work that they've done. I don't think they want to risk messing that up by causing any problems."

"You're probably right," Miss Dixie said, watching as Joanna put the lid on the chili and lifted it up, holding the bag that held the cheese in one hand along with one of the ladles.

"Are you ready?"

"I am," she said, grabbing the tea.

They made their way out of the house to the car where they set their food in a box that they had put in the back of the car for that purpose. They didn't have far to drive, but they didn't want to spill anything on the way there.

"How would you feel about going for ice cream this evening if the kids leave?" Joanna asked as she slid into the passenger seat and looked across at Miss Dixie who sat behind the wheel.

"I suppose that would be nice. You and me?" she said, sounding a little uncertain.

"Yeah. You and me. Since Whitney and Stonewall are going out, and we want to make sure that we give them plenty of space, and we don't want them to feel like we're just sitting at home twiddling our thumbs, bored out of our minds, and waiting for them to come back."

"Ha. I see. Well, that's a good strategy. Yeah. Let's go for ice cream."

Joanna smiled to herself. She and Miss Dixie seemed to be getting along better and better. As long as Joanna made sure that she was letting Miss Dixie know that Whitney and Stonewall had her full support, Miss Dixie had been very kind to her.

Even though the idea of Stonewall and Whitney's date had been looming in the back of her head like a doomsday prediction, she'd been trying to push those feelings aside and to be happy and supportive. That's what she wanted to be. To encourage Stonewall to make the most of this opportunity with Whitney, who seemed to be such a sweet girl.

Joanna had been curious as to whether or not Stonewall had talked to Whitney at all during the week, but she had not asked. Not wanting to tip her hand or accidentally say anything that would discourage him.

It wasn't long before they pulled up along the street at the rental and got the food out.

There had been some inexpensive bowls and silverware left in the house, and they had stocked dishwashing detergent so that all of the things they needed were in the house. She supposed they could have just cooked right in the house, but Miss Dixie was more comfortable in her own kitchen. But maybe, if they were here for another few weeks, she might suggest to Miss Dixie to come to the rental and cook. Regardless, Stonewall grinned huge when he saw them.

"I thought you guys got lost and were leaving me here to starve to death."

"Because you can't find a grocery store on your own," Joanna said, teasing, and then she thought maybe she was being a little bit too familiar, and she dipped her head down, pretending to study the floor so she didn't trip with the big pot of chili.

"Here. Let me carry that."

"Because you're afraid I'm going to drop it, or because you want to be the first to be able to dip into it?"

"Is that a trick question? Can the answer be both?"

"Joanna said you like cheese on your chili," his mother said, coming into the kitchen with them, setting the tea on the table, and then going directly to the cupboard to get some cups out for everyone.

"Joanna knows exactly how I like it. She didn't try to sneak any sour cream into it, did she?"

"She said you hated it," Miss Dixie said.

"All right. So she hasn't totally forgotten me in the amount of time that we've been separated this week. Which is probably more than we've ever been separated before in our lives," he said, looking at Joanna like he wanted her to agree with him.

She had to. This past week had been the most amount of time that she had spent away from Stonewall since her family had homeschooled him, and tonight would be even worse, because he would be with someone else. But she wasn't supposed to be jealous, because she was just supposed to be his friend.

"It has," she said simply, aware that Miss Dixie was watching her.

Miss Dixie cleared her throat. "Have you been talking to Whitney this week?"

Joanna almost laughed. Miss Dixie had no idea that she was asking that very question that Joanna wanted to ask herself.

"She texted me one night this week. Tuesday night? Maybe Wednesday. I'm not sure. She said hi, and I said hi, and that was it." Stonewall spoke like it wasn't a big deal as he grabbed bowls and playfully shoved Joanna out of the way as she grabbed silverware from the drawer.

She wanted to shove him back, but she wasn't going to do it in front of Miss Dixie.

"What? Afraid you're going to get in trouble?" Stonewall leaned down and whispered in her ear on his way to the table. It happened so quickly she didn't have a chance to react or to reply.

Not that she would have with Miss Dixie standing there looking at them. He didn't understand that she was walking a very tight line. She wanted to continue to be kind of a friend, but she also wanted his mother to trust her and to realize that Joanna wanted the absolute very best for Stonewall, because Joanna was pretty sure that was what the relationship was based on, a shared love of Stonewall.

She wanted to stick her tongue out at him when their eyes met a few seconds later, but she refrained from doing that as well and just stuck her nose in the air and looked away.

He huffed out a breath, which made his mother look at him and gave Joanna time to slide to the table and start putting the silverware down, completely ignoring both of them.

They sat down at the table, and Stonewall said a short blessing, thanking God for the family that they were surrounded with, the kids they were able to help, and the food.

She listened to his deep voice, familiar and beloved, and wondered how much longer she was going to get to hear him pray over their food, talk to her and tease her, and laugh with her...do all the things.

Would she still have come on this trip if she had known that this was the way it was going to end? With her having to let go of him?

She knew she would have, because she would spend every second that she could with him, but that didn't make her heart ache any less or her stomach feel any more settled.

Still, she took some chili, sprinkling some cheese over it and trying to have a normal conversation. The idea that Stonewall hadn't done more than text Whitney had made her whole heart smile, but she couldn't let on of course. His mom had not been overly happy about that. That had been obvious from her reaction.

She tried to put all the gloomy thoughts out of her head and just enjoy the moment. Wasn't that what life was? Just enjoying the moments. And allowing God to work however He wanted and having complete and total confidence that God's way was the best way. Even if that meant that she would no longer see her best friend on a daily basis and would have to exit his life stage left.

Chapter Twenty-One

Stonewall pulled up to the small ranch-type house at the edge of town. When he'd taken her home last Sunday, she'd given him directions. He hadn't even thought about getting the address for Whitney's house until he had gotten in his truck and realized he had no idea where he was going. That's how little thought he had put into this. He put far more thought into Joanna's reaction if he were to tell her how he felt about her. And weighing whether or not it was worth losing the relationship. Part of him felt like perhaps he was going to lose his relationship with her anyway, if he continued to pursue one with Whitney, and it would be better for him to lay his cards out on the table and for Joanna to reject him than for him to just assume that she didn't want him and pursue after Whitney.

He slowly got out of the truck, still not sure that he was doing the right thing. A big part of him felt like he should have talked to Joanna first. That before he went out on a date with Whitney, let alone two, he should have at least tried to see whether there was a chance for anything to develop between Joanna and him.

He was still thinking about that when he walked up the walk with his hand raised to knock on the door. Before he could, it opened wide with a beaming Whitney on the other side.

Even a dunce like him could tell that she had put a lot of effort into her appearance. Her hair was piled up on top of her head with perfect ringlets cascading out all around, and her makeup seemed sparkly and fancy. Her outfit was the same, fancy, with a flowing blouse and a swishy skirt and boots with big heels on them.

She said, "Hey there! I looked forward to this all week. And I know you can get a little bit antsy with wondering whether there's going to be a kiss at the end of the date or not, so I decided that I would just start the date with one, and then we don't have to worry about it." And with that, she grabbed a hold of his face with both hands and pulled his head down to hers.

He managed to miss her lips, and they ended up with their lips smashed to each other's cheeks. At least he assumed it was her lips, since his cheek felt a little wet when he pulled his face from hers.

"Sorry about that. You took me by surprise. I think we missed." He hoped that she would laugh and not say that they should try again.

She dropped her hands from his cheeks, and he moved his arm to grab a hold of the door and just happened to block the path of her arm in case she wanted to raise it again.

He didn't realize he was going to have to have any defensive moves perfected. She didn't seem like that type of girl.

"No problem," she said, sounding like it was very much a problem. "You want to come in for a bit? Or should I grab my coat?"

"Why don't you go ahead and grab your coat? I'm starving."

"Oh, that's too bad. I was really hoping I could bring you in and show you my plant collection."

"I'm always happy to look at plants," he said, although the words felt forced out, because if he wasn't starving to death, he would be happy to look at plants, but since he was exceptionally hungry, he would really prefer to eat first, and then he would look at all the plants she wanted. And listen to her prattle on about them for as long as she felt like it.

Joanna would have realized he was hungry and wanted to eat first. She would never expect him to do anything without food in his stomach. She understood that that was akin to asking a car to run without gas.

Either Whitney didn't notice that he was starving or didn't notice that he was reluctant, because she smiled brightly and said, "Great. I buy myself a plant every time I need a reward. It was something I started when I started my last diet. And it's kept the pounds off." She laughed like it was funny, and he supposed in a way it was, but she didn't really need to diet. At least he didn't think so. But he didn't think it was appropriate for him to say that either.

Regardless, he reluctantly stepped in and closed the door behind him and followed her down the hall.

Whitney chattered on as she led him into a room filled with plants. She touched each plant lovingly as she told him how she had gotten it and what kind of plant it was and the care it took, why some plants were close to the window and why some plants weren't. She said she had other plants scattered throughout the house, and in hindsight, he supposed he had seen them as he had walked through. He didn't care about her plants. Not that plants weren't good, and the people who collected them were not interesting to him, it was just... He wanted to know what Joanna was doing. Were she and his mom having a good time with the kids? They weren't getting hurt or bullied in any way, were they? The meal was going well. Surely. He wanted to go check on them. Just to make sure.

He wasn't exactly scared, but they'd only known those kids a week, and he wanted to make sure that everything was going okay. They seemed like good kids who just needed someone to take an interest in them as they had done. As someone had done for him. Joanna.

What if he lost her? What if one of them flipped out and somehow hurt her? What if today was the last day he would ever get to spend with her?

His heart clutched at the thought, and he shoved his balled fists in his pockets to keep from running to the door and yanking it open and running out of the house.

"Don't you think so?"

The last thing that Whitney said hung in the air as he gradually realized the room had filled with silence and he was expected to answer her question.

If he were interested in her, shouldn't he be paying attention to her?

Shouldn't he be hanging on her every word? Shouldn't he admire the room that she'd made for herself, filled with plants and made to look beautiful. He looked around, realizing that it really was a pretty room. Filled with nice greenery and obviously the plants were lovingly taken care of.

"Do you have any animals? A dog or cat?" he asked, suddenly curious. He couldn't imagine life without animals. He'd been missing all of the animals on the farm since they'd come, and normally he and Joanna would have joked about calling home so someone could hold the phone up to the dog so they could talk to him and get their animal fix. Maybe walk out to the barnyard while they were at it and see the calves.

"No. Why?" Whitney said, sounding a little bit irritated. And of course, of course she would be irritated because he hadn't answered her question but had asked one of his own and rather rudely at that.

"I'm sorry. I...kind of was thinking about how some people have plants and some people have animals, and I was just wondering if you had animals, and I wasn't paying attention. I'm sorry. Would you mind repeating the question?"

He felt bad. He obviously was fumbling this whole date thing. And it was totally his fault. She was doing everything right. Trying to show a little piece of herself to help him be interested. But instead of him returning the favor and showing interest, he had totally spaced out and was thinking about another woman. It really wasn't fair to her.

"We don't need to talk about this anymore. Plants aren't your thing. Animals are, I take it?" she said, putting a smile on her face as she asked the question, then walked by him, pushing the door open and holding it for him, waiting until he walked out before closing it behind him.

"I guess I am kind of an animal guy, but I'm a farmer. I do work with plants. Although usually it's outside and on a large-scale basis." That's what farmers did, they planted, harvested, and put up food for the winter to feed their animals.

"I see. So my little room isn't of much interest to you."

"I didn't mean that. I'm sorry. I was preoccupied. I'll try to do better. I'm definitely looking forward to going out to eat. Did you pick a restaurant?"

She smiled and named a restaurant he didn't recognize. "It's in

Cheyenne. I hope you don't mind driving the two hours to get there. Otherwise, there isn't much between here and there."

Two hours? He was going to drive two hours before he could eat? And then he had to drive two hours back home.

At least he didn't have to worry about what in the world they were going to do all evening.

"No, that's fine." If he'd known that, he would have eaten with his mom and Joanna so that he wouldn't be dying of hunger the whole way.

"Are you ready to go?" he asked, trying not to sound too eager. He didn't relish the idea of driving two hours to get to a restaurant, and then the thought struck him that perhaps there would be a waiting list.

"Should I make a phone call so we can make a reservation?"

"You might want to do that. They're probably pretty busy on Friday night. But I told everyone at work today that I was going, and they're dying of jealousy."

"I bet."

"Not just because of the restaurant, but I showed them a picture of you. You, I think more than the food, were the topic of interest."

He tried not to grimace. Not that he cared whether she showed his photo to her coworkers, he just didn't want to be associated with her, because... Because he wasn't sure that this was what he wanted. In fact, he knew it wasn't what he really wanted, but he would make it work if he had to. But that hardly seemed fair to her if she was all in and he was just making it work.

"Oh. Interestingly, the school in Sweet Water needs a principal. I'm applying for the job this week. Isn't that close to where you live?" she asked as he walked to the door, and she put a coat on while he stood and waited for her.

"That's my town. I didn't realize the school needed a principal."

"Apparently the woman who was a principal there last year had a baby, and she's decided to stay home. That's what I gathered from my research online. It might not come to anything, but that's the whole reason that I got my master's degree, so that I could perhaps quit teaching and become a principal instead."

"Is that a more fulfilling job?" he asked as he opened the door and waited for her to go through.

"It pays more." She laughed. "I don't know how fulfilling it is."

"I see."

He didn't want to look at her like she was shallow, because she wasn't. She was a nice girl, woman, sweet and kind and considerate. And he had not done well by her.

He opened the truck door for her, and she looked at the step. "My goodness. I need a stepladder to get in here."

That was nothing compared to some of the trucks of the guys that he'd seen, but he laughed along with her and held out his hand, offering it to her to help her in.

"I think I need a crane," she said, giving him a look, then putting her hand in his.

He was not going to lift her up. That would be too awkward. Luckily she did manage to get up. It wasn't that high. But he waited until she was settled in her seat before he closed the door and walked around. He was not going to ask her out on another date. He'd already decided that. But that didn't mean that he couldn't try to make sure that she had a good time on this one.

Even though he had decided that, it took the first hour of the trip for him to try to figure out something that they could talk about that didn't make him stumble and mumble around. She had tried to talk about college and roommates and coworkers and interviews, none of which he knew much of anything about. Aside from coworkers, but he loved his. They were all mostly the Clybourn family and their spouses, and he couldn't think of anyone he'd rather work with. So he didn't have much in common with Whitney who had a varied cast of coworkers, some of whom weren't that great.

"So tell me about you and Joanna. It's interesting that the two of you are here together, yet you're not together. Right?" she asked. Her question seemed innocent. She looked at him with some kind of calculated speculation in her eyes like she was trying to figure out what in the world he was hiding.

She probably thought she was treading on neutral ground.

"We've been best friends forever. She...she was a friend to me when I really needed one, and then she introduced me to her family, and they kind of took me in. I feel like I'm part of the Clybourn clan. I guess I would have said that Joanna is like a sister to me, only better. But I've never really had a sister, and I don't think of her other sisters the same way I think of her."

He could talk about Joanna forever. He hoped Whitney didn't notice.

She didn't seem to. But at least she seemed to realize that it was a subject that she could discuss with him.

"The two of you seem to get along so well. You're just...really into each other. I can't believe that there's never been any kind of...romantic interest there?" she asked, pausing a little as though stumbling to get the right words.

"No. Never." Not until now. He felt a little bit guilty like he was lying, but it was the truth up until this trip that he had never been the slightest bit romantically interested in Joanna, and she hadn't been in him.

"Like you've never had any adolescent kisses or tried things out on each other?"

He drew back a bit and gave her a confused look, feeling his brows draw down clear over his eyes. "No?"

"All right. That look was very telling. I guess sometimes people try things for a little bit and realize that they're not meant to be together that way, and they let it go."

"I've heard of a lot of best friends doing that. That kind of ruins a relationship."

"Actually one of my coworkers was married to what she termed her best friend. They were high school sweethearts, friends all through elementary school. Now, they've been divorced for two years, and they can't talk to each other except through their lawyers. It was a terrible mistake, she says, and it ruined the best friendship she ever had."

"That's too bad." And just confirmed what he had been thinking all along. That being with Joanna, or trying to be, could be a huge mistake.

"But I have another coworker who also married her best friend, and she's the happiest married person I know. I would love to have a marriage just like hers. I don't think there's anyone in the school who disagrees with me. Hands down, her marriage is awesome."

"Yeah. I can see how that would happen." He knew he didn't sound overly enthusiastic. He couldn't. Because he was thinking too hard. Was that what he was going to miss? The kind of marriage that would make everyone who knew him wish that they had that kind of marriage? If he knew for sure that was going to happen, he would turn the truck around, no matter how hungry he was, and drive straight back to Joanna, and make her give him a chance to show her that he could be a husband as well as her best friend.

Unfortunately, there were no guarantees for that kind of thing in life, and he just didn't know.

"How do you really feel about Joanna?" Whitney asked after a little while.

He glanced over at her, only to find her staring at him speculatively.

What was he going to say?

He really didn't know. He didn't want to lie, but this was a date, and he couldn't hardly tell his date that he had feelings for another woman, could he?

"I've always felt nothing but friendship and like she was a sibling, a really close, good sibling. But a sibling nonetheless. Until about two weeks ago. For some reason, her brother, Ezra, said to me that best friends sometimes make the best life partners. I don't know what it was about that, because I'd heard that a million times before, but... I guess it got me thinking that maybe Joanna would make a good life partner."

He was afraid he had said too much. He took a deep breath and then looked across the seat. "Please don't say anything to her. I certainly haven't. And... I certainly haven't acted on that in any way. I came here because my mom wanted me to take you out on a few dates and get to know you. And I said I would do that. That's what I'm doing."

"I admire a man who keeps his word. Especially his word to his mother. That's important."

"Thank you. I admire people like that too. I've aspired to be someone like that."

"It looks to me like you are meeting your aspirations."

"What about you? Has there ever been a special someone in your life?" He wasn't particularly interested, but he wanted to get the spotlight off himself. He felt like he just said too much. And she hadn't promised not to say anything to Joanna. If she wanted to, she could really ruin things between them. Or at least try to. But Whitney didn't seem like that kind of person.

"Once, a long time ago, I spent some time with someone I really liked. Really, really liked. But he was a lot different than I was, and I guess you could say his life trajectory was going in a different direction than mine. And we...parted ways, amicably, but parted nonetheless, and I haven't seen or talked to him since." She paused, and then she ran her hands over the top of her purse, almost absentmindedly like she didn't realize what she was doing. "I know he is the kind of man that anyone would want to be with. Honest and upright. A man with integrity and... Maybe we'll meet again someday." She gave him a little smile. It seemed forced.

They drove for a few miles in silence until she finally said, "I get the impression you have feelings for Joanna. I've felt like that almost since you first came."

"I don't have feelings for her. I mean, I don't know what I feel for her."

"I believe that. I believe you don't know. But I kinda thought that maybe it wasn't a serious thing, and if you truly aren't interested in her, that maybe we could make something work. You're exactly the kind of guy that I would really like to have. But I don't think I'll ever have you, because I think Joanna always will."

He didn't say anything to that. He wasn't sure what to say. She could very well be right. "I promised my mom—"

She put a hand up. "I know. I actually told your mom that I would go out with you and try to make things work out too. She really would like some grandkids, and she'd like to know you're happily settled before she dies."

"She's not gonna die for a really long time."

"You don't know. Anyone of us could die at any time. You just never know."

"When she does, she's not going to care."

"That's a little bit disrespectful, I think," she said, sounding like he might have offended her. Joanna would have laughed.

"Sorry," he mumbled, keeping his eyes on the road. He was so used to Joanna, anything different just wasn't right.

"Anyway. If you don't mind, so that we can both keep our word to your mother, we'll go out tonight, we'll enjoy each other's company. We'll just assume that we're going to be friends. And we can go out one more time? Just so your mom can't say that we didn't give it a good shot."

"Really?" he asked, looking across the seat at her. She was going to do exactly what he would have suggested they do, just to keep his mom happy. If they went out on three different dates, they would be keeping their word, and doing what they said, and could honestly say that there just wasn't a spark and things didn't work out. No one could say that they hadn't tried.

"Yes. Really. We'll try, and I'm pretty sure that nothing's going to develop, and we'll part friends. No hard feelings, and your mom will be happy."

"That sounds great. I really appreciate you being so big about it."

"I appreciate you trying. I am trying not to feel like a failure, like there's a problem with me, because I know there's not. It's just...so hard to find a good guy."

"Yeah. I guess it's hard to find the right one, one that you think will stick with you for the rest of your life." He had no doubt Joanna would. He knew for a fact that she did whatever she said she was going to do, and there wasn't a person in the world more loyal than she. If only he could get her to see him the way he saw her.

It seemed almost impossible, as much as she'd been stiff-arming him lately.

"You won't say anything to Joanna about what I said to you?"

She looked surprised. "Aren't you going to say something to her?"

He sat for a moment, focusing on the yellow line flowing by. "You remember what you said about the couple that had been best friends, got married, and were divorced and now don't speak to each other at all?"

"Yes?"

"That's my fear. I don't want that to become Joanna and me. I would rather be best friends for the rest of my life and have her with me than take the risk of developing it into something more and losing everything."

"But what you get could be so much better than what you have. Isn't that worth the risk?"

"I don't think so," he said, thinking that he was right. He would rather have Joanna forever than lose her trying to make what they had better. He wasn't sure that it would be possible to make what they had better, although there was definitely a part of him that figured that a physical relationship on top of their solid friendship would probably be about the best thing that could ever happen to anyone.

"You do realize that the other couple I told you about has a relationship that most people only dream about."

And that's exactly what he was thinking. He could have that with Joanna, he was almost sure. But if he was wrong, he would lose it all.

"Yeah. I get it."

"Why don't you just try? I think that you and Joanna are not the kind of people that are going to hate each other so much that you can't talk except through your lawyers. That's a pretty extreme case."

"Yeah." Extreme or no, it was possible, and he hated that idea.

Chapter Twenty-Two

"You guys are going on another date?" Joanna asked, trying to swallow the lump that formed in her throat when Stonewall had said he'd be going out again with Whitney. It was Saturday morning, and they were hoping that the kids showed up to work the entire day. They had a lot of food planned, and the idea that they were teaching them valuable skills that they might be able to use on other jobs was exciting as well. One of the kids had mentioned that they should get together and form some kind of work detail, where they hired out to the people in town to do odd jobs.

Joanna thought it was an awesome idea, and she loved the way he thought.

"Yeah. We decided next week we'd go on another one."

"This one must have gone pretty well if you guys are doing another one."

"I guess it was okay." Stonewall didn't seem to want to talk about it. Which was odd. Usually there weren't too many things they had a problem talking about, unless he was thinking about something and needed to figure it out in his head before he put it out in words to the world, the way he said it.

"Whitney said she might show up today too," he said casually.

"Oh. That's great. The more the merrier," she said, although her words belied the feeling of her stomach sinking down to her kneecaps and hanging there.

Whitney was coming? Were they that close now that Whitney was going to spend Saturdays with them too? Like it wasn't already bad enough that they were going out on another date next weekend.

No. This is what she wanted. She was happy for them.

At least she tried to tell herself that.

"Here, you take this, and I'll go over here and measure this for the board we were talking about yesterday," Stonewall said as he handed her the end of the tape measure.

She got a hold of it, but it wasn't a very good hold and she accidentally let go. It was an older tape measure, and it snapped back, smacking him in the back of the head.

He stopped and turned around slowly, his eyes narrowed.

"Oops?" she said, grinning a bit. She knew it hadn't really hurt him.

"You did that on purpose, didn't you?"

"I would never!" she said, shrugging and trying to look innocent.

He growled, took two steps back, and before she knew it, he had her over his shoulder. He hadn't done that for years, and she squealed, not pretending.

"That's it. I've had enough of your attitude, I'm going to—"

He stopped abruptly and froze. Joanna peeked out from behind his waist, looking underneath his arm and seeing an upside-down Whitney standing frozen in the doorway.

Oops. That was not exactly how she had wanted to greet Whitney today. And that was definitely not something she wanted to get back to Miss Dixie.

She started to struggle so that he would put her down, and he started at the same time to set her down, and somehow her hand got tangled up with his knee and her foot got caught somewhere so that when she slid off his shoulder, she ended up landing on the floor on her butt and somehow taking him down with her.

He landed on top of her with the grunt that matched her "Oof!"

That wasn't much better than her over his shoulder with them all tangled together, and Joanna tried to get up, struggling, until Stonewall said, "Just relax. We'll get our feet untangled before we start stepping on each other to get up."

"I'm sorry. I just panicked a little because...Whitney," she said softly, hoping Whitney couldn't hear.

He shook his head. "It's okay. We weren't doing anything wrong." He said that with so much confidence she almost believed him. But normal people didn't run around hanging over each other's shoulders and carrying each other around and rolling around on the floor together. Which was what it looked like, even though that wasn't exactly what was going on.

He got their legs straightened out, and then they grabbed each other's hands and stood up using their weight to counterbalance each other. They'd done that so often that it was almost second nature, but she didn't stop to look in his eyes and grin and laugh the way she normally would have. Instead, she went around him and hurried over to the door where Whitney still stood. She didn't look quite as angry as what Joanna would have expected her to, considering that she was going out on a third date with Stonewall next week.

"I'm sorry. Stonewall and I were just goofing off the way we always do. It wasn't really what it looked like."

"Oh? What did it look like?" Whitney asked, her eyes blinking, and maybe there was a little tone of annoyance in her voice.

"I... I don't know. I guess I just assumed that... We're just friends."

"That's what you keep saying," Whitney said, and then she didn't say anything else.

"Hey there, Whitney," Stonewall said, coming up and seeming to hesitate for a moment before he leaned forward and bussed her cheek.

That made Joanna absolutely insane to consider whether or not he might have kissed her good night the night before.

Maybe they had done more than just kiss. She blocked those thoughts from her head. Whether they did or whether they didn't was none of her business, and she was not going to think about it. That way just lay aggravation and insanity, and she didn't need that in her life. She would just focus on what she could do, and that was help the kids as they came in and serve wherever she could.

137

"I came to help. You can put me to work," Whitney said as Stonewall leaned back, and Joanna tried to corral her raging thoughts.

"Joanna and I were just trying to measure for a board that needs to be cut over here, and if you'd like, the room on the other side is done. You can sweep that up. There's a shop vac downstairs. If you can't get it up the stairs, I can do it for you."

"All right." Whitney turned to go, and then she stopped and gasped, her hand going to her throat and one trembling word coming out of her mouth. "Stonewall?"

Joanna looked up to see that Declan had arrived. He did look a little scary with his eyebrow piercings and the tattoo that went down his throat. He wasn't eighteen, and some kind of guardian or parent must have signed for it. It made him look older, especially with the long hair that hung around his collar and the baggy jeans and untied boots that clumped at his feet.

"Whitney, this is Declan, and he will give you a hand with that shop vac."

"He helps you?" Whitney said, turning around and looking at Stonewall like he was daft.

"He does. He's a good help."

"I know him from school," Whitney said, turning back around. She seemed to be trying to gather her professional armor around her like a cloak, but she obviously did not have a good impression of Declan, whatever he had done at school.

"Then you know he's a pretty hard worker, and he does a great job. He's good with the details," Stonewall said, sounding offhanded, but Joanna wasn't fooled. He was leading Whitney into Declan's strengths and telling her that she needed to encourage him in those areas.

"Well, then great. Good to know that he's good with details. Sounds to me like you would be good with math," she said. Then, lifting her chin, she looked at Declan. "Show me what this shop vac thing is. And carry it for me. I might need you to show me how to use it as well."

"Yes, ma'am," Declan said, giving Stonewall and Joanna a wide-eyed glance, kind of like he'd been caught red-handed doing something bad by the teacher, and now he was headed to the principal's office.

Joanna had to laugh after they left, but she did it quietly. And then she sobered immediately, remembering what Whitney had walked in on.

"I'm really sorry about earlier. I did not mean for Whitney to walk in on that. If your mom finds out—"

"Whitney is not going to tell her." Stonewall said this with such confidence that Joanna was taken aback. He knew her that well?

"Okay. If you say so."

"Trust me. Whitney is not going to go tattle to my mom about you."

She had a hard time believing that, but she didn't want to talk bad about Whitney, since Stonewall was obviously infatuated with her. But was it really going to matter whether she had a good relationship with Stonewall's mother or not? Especially if she and Stonewall were never together again. So she closed her mouth and jerked her head.

She took a breath and took a step away, but stopped when she felt Stonewall's hand on her arm.

"Joanna?"

"Yeah?" she asked, trying to keep her voice light and normal, but she didn't turn around.

"What's wrong?"

"Nothing."

"Joanna."

"If you say that Whitney is not going to say anything, then that's fine. I believe you. And if she does, if you and Whitney get together, it's not going to matter if your mom is mad at me."

"It means that much to you that my mom not be mad at you?"

"She's your mom. She's the closest family that you have in the world. Of course I want to be in a good relationship with her. I've tried every time we've been around her, but this is the first time that I feel like I found something that I can work with her on."

"What's that?"

"Your happiness. Getting you and Whitney together. Your mom and I kind of have a conspiracy going, and she's actually been being very nice to me. So nice, in fact, that I could hardly believe it. If she finds out about today, I can probably kiss that relationship goodbye."

"When the relationship is based on something as superficial as that, maybe it's not much."

"You're right. It's not much. But it's better than anything I ever had." She didn't know how to explain to him why it was so important to her to have a good relationship with his mother. But she figured he probably got it. He was just giving her a hard time because it really was superficial. Still, it was a start.

"Never mind. If you and Whitney get together, it's not going to matter what kind of relationship I have with your mom. Let's get this measuring tape and get this figured out." She was not going to dwell on it. She was going to do the best she could and allow God to work everything else out.

Chapter Twenty-Three

What were they doing right now?

Joanna moved from the window in her bedroom at Miss Dixie's house and walked to the bed, then back to the window, standing there, crossing her arms over her chest, and thinking about the almost full moon. It was romantic. It would make for a very romantic date for Stonewall and Whitney.

She tried to be happy about that.

She had eaten supper with Dixie, and they had gone for ice cream which seemed to become their habit when Stonewall and Whitney went out for a date. She had a good time, and she really did like Dixie. She was a nice lady and truly wanted the best for her son. Dixie had wanted to talk about Whitney and how wonderful she was and how perfect Stonewall and she were together, and Joanna tried to be as excited and interested as she was supposed to be, but she was finding it harder and harder to pretend, because that's what it was, pretending.

She shoved her hands in her jammy pants pockets and tried to convince herself that she was getting sleepy enough to get into bed and go to sleep. But it was only nine o'clock, and she wanted to talk to Stonewall.

She no sooner thought that than her phone rang.

Excited that it might be Stonewall calling her, she hurried to where it sat on the charger on the nightstand only to see it was Priscilla.

Swallowing her disappointment, she pulled the charger out and swiped to answer.

"Hello?" She hadn't talked to Priscilla for a while, although she'd texted various family members every day. Making sure that everything on the ranch was okay, that her special bottle babies were being taken care of, and that someone was watering the two plants that she had on her side of their duplex.

"Joanna. I didn't get you out of bed, did I?"

"We're not on the farm. But... I do have my jammies on."

"Oh. I didn't realize until the phone was ringing that it was nine o'clock, and Mom and Dad said it was never a good idea to call a farmer after eight."

"I agree with that. But you didn't wake me up, so you don't have to worry about it," she said easily, wondering what Priscilla needed.

"Do you have a minute?"

"I sure do." She tried to push her own troubles away. Priscilla had more than enough troubles for three people, and she didn't want to load her up with hers.

"I was just wondering how things were going."

"I was kind of expecting to see you here."

"I don't think I'm gonna make it until just before you guys leave, unless you leave early."

"So you're still coming?"

"Yeah. I've spoken with my ex, and we might be able to work out a custody arrangement that will make it so we don't have to go through the courts. But you never know with him."

"Yeah. I'm sorry that things have been so hard for you. I didn't guess when you guys got married that he would be such a jerk."

"Me either. Trust me, I definitely wouldn't have married him if I would've realized he was going to leave me." Her voice sounded sad but resigned.

Joanna stared out the window, looking at the moon, thinking how many times the moon had shone down on people who thought they were going to be together forever, and then it just didn't work out. It was sad. And she didn't want that to be her. She didn't want it to be Stonewall either, and there was a nagging part of her that said that if Stonewall and Whitney got married, they would stay together forever, but they wouldn't be happy.

"Joanna?"

"Yeah?"

"I was just wondering about you and Stonewall."

Joanna froze, her breath caught in her throat. "What about us?"

"You've always said that you're just friends."

"Yes," she said cautiously, because that's what they'd always said. They were just friends.

"I was just wondering if the idea of Stonewall being with someone else has...changed your mind."

That seemed kind of intuitive. Joanna sighed. "You have enough on your mind. I guess I am kinda conflicted, but I don't want to burden you."

"You know how nice it would be to have someone else's problems to think about for a little bit?" Priscilla laughed. "You can't even begin to imagine how much I wish I could think about someone else's problems."

"All right. How's this? Stonewall's mom is set on having Stonewall and Whitney get together, and she's been mean to me forever."

"I remember her being unkind to you. Not terrible, just...not nice."

"Yeah. Well, now that I'm kind of on her side, quote, unquote, in that I'm helping Stonewall and Whitney get together, she and I have actually developed a...kind of good relationship, but a relationship nonetheless."

"Wow. That doesn't sound like a problem."

"It's not. Except... You're right. The more Stonewall is with Whitney, the more I want him for myself. Is that one of those cases of wanting something you can't have?"

"I guess there are cases like that. Though I never wanted my ex when he was with someone else. I mean, the moment he cheated on me, I was totally done with him. I suppose I would've taken him back for the kids, but he's married now, and that would mean another divorce, and I definitely do not want that. And even more, I don't want him. I don't want a cheater."

"Totally understood. But yeah, I guess that's my issue. I'm all edgy right now, and that's why I'm in my jammies but I'm not in bed snoring away. I'm thinking about them. Did he kiss her? What was he like? Did he hold her hand? Are they laughing together? Are they doing all the things that we did? I'm acting like a jealous girlfriend, and yet I never had those kinds of feelings for him. It's...weird."

"And hard. Sounds like it's very hard."

"It is. I want to go bursting in on their date, break it up, grab her by her hair, and yank her out. And the problem is, Whitney is such a sweet, kind, considerate person that I would feel terrible doing anything like that to her, but...I just want him."

"And did you tell him?"

"No way!"

"Why not?"

"Well, I told you about his mom, first off."

"So? So what if she decides she hates you. If you have Stonewall for the rest of your life, it would be worth it."

"I don't know. If I have Stonewall, I'm going to want to have a good relationship with his mom. But if his mom hates me because she wanted Whitney, then I'm never going to have a good relationship with her."

"Does Stonewall seem to like Whitney?"

"I guess. I don't know. He's gone out on three dates with her. I mean, this was the third one. After the second one, I felt like I was going to die when he said they were going out on another one this weekend."

"Does he spend a lot of time texting or talking to her?"

"I don't know. The first week, he didn't. He said he just said hi, and she said hi, and then they didn't say anything more. And I didn't ask him about this week, because I couldn't stand the answer."

"I thought you're going to say you were too busy working to ask something like that."

"I wish. I haven't been too busy working. And this kind of work is not the kind of work that engages your brain. You can sit there and think about all the problems in your life while you're hammering nails and using the impact gun."

"That is one nice thing about carpentry work. You have all that time to think. Or I guess you could look at it like that's the bad thing about it. You have all that time to think."

"Yeah. Exactly."

"So you're just going to let her have him? You're not going to tell him how you feel?"

"I'm not sure exactly how I feel. I mean, you could be right. Now that I can't have him, I want him. Or maybe it's just the idea that he's my best friend and I know that he's not going to be my best friend anymore. It's not a romantic thing, it's just a friend thing."

"Are you attracted to him?"

"How do you tell?"

"Well, let me just preface this by saying, I don't really think you need to be attracted to someone in order to marry them."

"Really?" It was something that she heard a lot before, but she wasn't sure whether she agreed with that or not.

"Yeah. I guess that's a nice thing. But attraction fades. When you get used to someone, it's not like the burning hot attraction that you have for your new boyfriend or whatever. It burns down to a simmer, and you... I don't know, I just don't think attraction is something to build a life on. It's almost like lust, it fades, and if it doesn't have anything solid underneath it, you end up with nothing."

"I suppose you're right. I suppose that's what I believe too. But... You asked me if I was attracted to Stonewall?"

"Yeah. Have you ever thought about kissing him? Do you find that your eyes get caught on him and you have trouble looking away? Do you want to hold his hand or touch him even when you don't have to?"

Joanna thought about that for a while. She never really dreamed about kissing him, but she liked touching him. Even when they were just friends, they would goof off, and his touch had a comfort in it that no one else's did. She definitely wouldn't label it attraction though.

"You're not saying anything," Priscilla said, saying it almost like a question.

"I'm trying to think of whether or not I would like to kiss Stonewall." The answer was yes. Yes, she would like to kiss Stonewall. She would like for him to put his arms around her and hold her tight, and she didn't even think it would be that awkward. Not for her. Not unless he didn't want to.

"And?" Priscilla prodded when she didn't say anything.

"I think the only thing that would be awkward about it would be if he didn't want to. And then I would be devastated. More devastated than I would be if we lost our friendship. You know?"

"If you lost your friendship?"

"Because he got married to someone else. Because he can't really be good friends with me, or best friends with me anyway, and have another woman in his life. What woman is going to want some man to have his best friend hanging around?"

"Some men have their best friend, a female, be the best man at a wedding."

"Do you think those are really good marriages?" Joanna asked, already knowing the answer in her head.

"No. I think you're right. I don't think they would be good marriages. Whether they're just friends or not, I do think a man should have his wife in a place of honor that is incomparable to any other woman in his life. Even his best friend or his secretary."

"What do you think I should do?" Joanna asked, feeling like she was tired of thinking about it, tired of worrying about what Whitney and Stonewall were doing, tired of feeling like she was losing her best friend, and wishing that she could make him want her the way she wanted him. But that was the problem. She couldn't make him want her when he wanted Whitney, and she wouldn't want to try. She truly did, as much as she was saying that she was doing it to have a good relationship with Miss Dixie, want Stonewall to be happy.

"I think you should tell him. I think you should lay your feelings out there and see what he says."

"But what if he doesn't like me the way I like him?"

"Then you'll know it. You'll know exactly how he feels, and you won't wonder about it the rest of your life."

"But I'll be devastated."

"You'll be devastated, but you'll know that you did everything you could, and he just didn't want to. If you don't do it, you'll always wonder."

"But I might ruin our relationship."

"You say that, and it's true, but if he doesn't want you and he wants Whitney, your relationship is going to change anyway, and you said yourself you're going to step back. So, you have just as much of a chance of making your relationship even better as you do of ruining it."

Joanna took a deep breath and leaned her forehead against the cool glass of the window, staring at the moon, wondering if she had the guts to do what Priscilla had just told her she should.

She wanted to say that she would pray about it, but she felt like that was a copout because she wasn't sure she was going to pray. Did she want to know what God wanted? Would He even tell her? Sometimes she prayed and it seemed like God didn't answer. Like either way was acceptable to Him. This wasn't a matter of right or wrong. Stonewall wasn't committed to Whitney in any way, so she wasn't coming in and breaking up a committed relationship. Let alone a husband-and-wife relationship. So she could tell him if she wanted to, and it wouldn't be wrong. But she could also keep her mouth shut and let Stonewall move ahead. Giving him room and space.

"I guess I don't see a problem with either way. Like both ways are okay."

"Then do the way that you want. Unless you feel like the Lord is telling you a definite no, lay things out for Stonewall and see what he says." She heard Priscilla's sigh over the phone. "Listen to me. Like I'm the expert on relationships. I'm not. Maybe you should just ignore me and do the exact opposite of what I would do. That would probably be smarter."

"I don't know about that. You've gained a lot of wisdom through the trials that you've been through. Not that I would want to go through those trials just to gain that wisdom. But I respect the pain you've been through and the knowledge and wisdom you gained."

"Thanks," Priscilla said, although her tone was subdued, almost depressed.

"Thanks for talking to me. I... I guess it's always easier to figure out what you're thinking when you lay it out in a conversation and you have someone else's opinion."

"I don't want to see you hurt, but I also don't want to see you lose

Stonewall. You and he are...perfect together. I don't know if I've ever seen two people more perfect together than you. Other than maybe Ezra and Alaska, but they certainly don't look like they would be perfect together."

"They don't, do they?" Joanna asked, thinking of her serious older brother and the sweet, tattooed Alaska. They really were perfect.

As perfect as Stonewall and she?

She wasn't sure, but she knew that she wanted to do something about it. But whether or not she would, she wasn't sure.

Chapter Twenty-Four

"What do we have here?" Stonewall said as Declan walked to the doorway of the room, a little girl at his side.

"This is Lolly. Sometimes I see her hanging around, and she follows me. She wanted to know where we went all the time and why it seemed like we were always having so much fun." He ruffled the hair of the little girl standing beside him. The hair was cut short, but the face was too pixie-like to be a boy.

"I think she also wants food."

Stonewall nodded, smiling. It was Saturday afternoon, and they'd bought pizza for lunch. Everyone had hung around eating, and a few people, like Declan, had continued to stay and work.

"What did you say her name was?" Joanna asked, coming to the doorway behind Declan. She had deliberately avoided Stonewall all day today. She hadn't asked about his date and had barely greeted him when she had walked in, later than usual and after the teens had gotten there. Stonewall figured it was probably on purpose.

"It's Lolly," the little girl piped up, looking admiringly up at Joanna. "Can I have pizza?"

Joanna smiled. "I'd love to get you some pizza. And you can have as much as you want," she said, and then she held her hand out after a little hesitation, as though she wasn't sure whether the little girl felt like she was too big to hold someone's hand.

The little girl didn't hesitate at all. She grabbed onto Joanna's hand and skipped off beside her.

Stonewall watched her go. Whitney was the one who was a schoolteacher, and he supposed Whitney was good with children, but Joanna had always had a way about her that had children trusting her immediately.

She would be an excellent mother. And Stonewall wondered what their children would look like.

Where had that thought come from? No. He wasn't going to wonder about things like that. Although, last night had been the finale between him and Whitney. They had agreed to just be friends. Now he just needed to tell his mother. Which he figured he would do tomorrow over Sunday dinner. He hadn't yet told her that he was going to be at her house for Sunday dinner instead of taking Whitney somewhere.

He could imagine that his mother was not going to be very happy, but he was determined that he was not going to be with Joanna until he told his mother, just so his mother wouldn't get any ideas that it was somehow Joanna's fault.

Once he had that straightened out, which he figured was going to take some doing, he was going to pursue Joanna, not as a friend, but as more.

Because that's how he felt. And if she didn't feel that way, well... Maybe he wasn't going to think about that.

About the time he made up his mind that he was going to do it, he figured that he didn't want to risk it and he would rather just be friends with her for the rest of his life.

He would really like to have someone older and wiser to talk to, and Ezra's face flitted through his head.

"Would you mind taking over in here?" he asked Declan who had deposited the supplies that he had been carrying into the corner of the room and had started to walk back out.

"I can. Something wrong?"

"I have to make a phone call," he said and then didn't say anything more.

Joanna was somewhere in the house, and there were kids all through it, so he decided he would walk outside and up to the playground he'd seen multiple times as he'd driven by.

He didn't run into anyone as he was walking out, although he did walk past the opening to the kitchen where Joanna had Lolly sitting in a chair, a plate of pizza in front of her and a glass of milk sitting beside her. The kid looked as happy as she could be, and Joanna was talking to her a mile a minute. Joanna could talk to anyone and was comfortable with anyone as well.

He missed that. Missed having her by his side, knowing where she was every second and what was going on with her as well. Whitney had suggested that maybe Joanna had her eye on someone and would be making a move once Stonewall had settled down. She had suggested that maybe Joanna hadn't wanted to leave him before he had found the one that he wanted.

He didn't think that was true, but it could be.

He waited until he had made it all the way to the park and made sure that it was empty. Sitting down on a bench over by the side, where he would be out of the way in case someone came to play, he dialed Ezra's number. Ezra would never mind talking to him and would always take time if he could.

It went straight to voicemail.

He walked all of this way, stoked up for conversation, and then felt the letdown of having his call not be answered.

But he could call Caleb. Caleb was fourth in birth order, after Ezra and then the twins Phoebe and Priscilla. Caleb was a little bit more good-natured, more prone to smiling, and to hear the siblings tell it, he was an imp as a child, getting into more scrapes than any of the other kids put together. Stonewall had put two and two together and deduced that Caleb had been a bit of a wild child, maybe had a few skeletons in his closet, but he was on the straight and narrow and hadn't wavered for years, not that Stonewall had known, and Stonewall knew everything that went on in the Clybourn family.

After a couple more minutes of thought, he dialed Caleb's number.

"Hello?" Caleb answered on the first ring.

"Hey there. What's up?" Stonewall said, like he was just calling to shoot the breeze.

"Not much. I just tagged a calf, and I'm wishing you and Joanna hadn't left, because this mama almost got me."

"I see. So in your warped sense of the world, it's better for that crazy mama to almost kill Joanna and me than it is for her to almost get you?"

"Yep."

Stonewall huffed out a laugh. "Good to know, bro."

"You know I love you," Caleb said easily, and Stonewall could picture him, leaning against the four-wheeler, one arm pulled over his chest, the other holding his phone to his ear, looking out over the cows in the lush green pasture with the brilliant North Dakota sky in the background, just enjoying the weather and breeze and the sun and having a friendly conversation. Caleb was definitely relaxed and willing to take a break to talk.

"I need some advice, and Ezra didn't answer his phone."

"I'm your second choice. And that's supposed to somehow make me feel happy?" Caleb teased.

"You're my first choice, since my first choice isn't available."

"That doesn't even make sense."

"I know."

"What's up? You're in some kind of financial difficulty?"

"No." He stopped. "What made you ask that?"

"I'm trying to think what would make you call and need advice. Surely you're not in a burning building. Because if you are, let's cut to the chase."

"No. I'm sitting on a park bench, thinking about children and realizing that I want that to happen with Joanna."

"You're gonna marry her first, right?" Caleb said, and while there was still teasing in his tone, his words were a little bit sharp, like Stonewall was going to be in trouble if he didn't.

"Of course." He sighed, blew out a breath, and hooked one hand behind his neck, trying to figure out how to say what he needed to. "I'm not sure how she feels about me. Whether she feels the same way, and if I should even try to see if she does."

"But your mom had a girl for you. Did you decide you didn't want that one?"

"I never did. Yeah, I took her out on three dates to make my mom happy, and tomorrow I'm going to tell my mom that it didn't work out between us. Joanna has been cultivating a relationship with my mom, and the only way she's been able to do that is to pretend to be on board with Whitney and me getting together. So I can't pursue Joanna until I tell my mom about Whitney and me. I haven't even told Joanna that."

"I'm a little bit confused, this sounds kinda convoluted, and I feel like I should pass the phone along to one of my sisters to help you."

"Shut up."

"I thought you wanted me to give you advice."

"This feels like a huge mistake."

"Tell Joanna how you feel."

"Are you saying that to get rid of me?"

"I would never," Caleb said, sounding like he totally would.

"Is that really what you think I should do? Because I'm honestly not sure."

"What do you have to lose by telling her how you feel?"

"I could lose our friendship forever."

"Really? You think Joanna is going to...break up with you and not be your friend anymore because you wanted to know whether she wanted to have babies with you?"

"Yeah."

"Okay. I would say it a little bit more delicately than that. Ask her if she's ever thought about you guys being more. Or if you're going to be a real man about it, you can tell her you've been thinking about you guys being more and ask her what she thinks about it, that way she doesn't have to say her feelings first."

"I'm not sure if I'm a 'real' man or not," Stonewall said, feeling one side of his mouth turn up. Caleb was a hoot and a riot, but he was no dummy either. "By the way, I've never thought about this, but why haven't you gotten married?"

"What did you say the name of the girl was that your mom's trying to set you up with?"

"Whitney."

"That's why."

Stonewall blinked. What was Caleb saying? He opened his mouth to ask but didn't get any words out before Caleb spoke.

"I've got to go. Tell her how you feel. Ask her how she feels. Don't sit around wondering or worrying or ruminating about something that could be even better if you just took a leap of faith."

"All right. Thanks."

They hung up, but Stonewall didn't get up right away. There was a little bit of a mystery there with Caleb. Was it the Whitney that Stonewall had been with? Or was it a different Whitney? Or was he talking about something completely different? Was it something Whitney said that made him realize that he didn't want to get married?

He could ask Joanna about that. But he and Joanna weren't exactly on easy terms anymore. Him dating Whitney had really put the skids to that. Or maybe it was him saying that they were going to be separated anyway, so they might as well get used to it. That had seemed to have been hard for her as well. Did she think it was easy for him?

He wanted to go to her right away, wanted to talk to her, figure things out, but he didn't. He didn't want to rush it. Not with his mother in the picture, and if Joanna said yes to him, he definitely wanted his mother on board, and he wanted her on good terms with Joanna. Particularly since Joanna said that was important to her. It had always been whatever was important to Joanna was important to him too.

He stood slowly, looking around the playground again. Funny how he hadn't thought about children much at all in his life, unless he was required to take care of them, like he and Joanna often had with her nieces and nephews, but as for having any of his own, he hadn't considered it. Now, looking at the playground equipment, he could see Joanna and him bringing their children here to have a fun Saturday afternoon. Spending time doing repair work with their own kids, raising them the way Joanna's family had been raised, with a lot of love and laughter and hard work mixed in between to make everything balanced and right.

Joanna would be an amazing mom, and he had a lot of great

examples that he could follow to try to make sure that he wasn't a terrible father.

Maybe his mom would even move to North Dakota.

But there he was getting ahead of himself. He wasn't going to build a whole fantasy on something that he didn't even know was going to happen. But he was going to find out. He needed to say something to Joanna. Beating around the bush wasn't his style, and being afraid was wrong. The Bible said God did not give a spirit of fear.

With that determination in his heart and the knowledge that he needed to talk to his mother at Sunday lunch first, he started back toward the rental.

Chapter Twenty-Five

"I'll see you tomorrow maybe?" Joanna said as Lolly smiled up at her, clutching Declan's hand.

The little girl nodded, her short hair waving a bit in the breeze created by the movement of her head.

Joanna had thought about asking the little girl to go to church, but maybe she would do that next week. She didn't even know who the kid's parents were, and she wanted to talk to Declan about her a little bit first.

She felt a tendril of loneliness try to creep in on her as Declan walked away with the girl. She didn't know where Stonewall had gone. She only knew that he had left a while ago. It was funny, she might not be working side by side with him, but she was hyperaware of what he was doing. And she had known almost the second he had left.

The pizza had been cleaned up in the kitchen, and the sun was just now setting over the horizon.

Normally she would be thinking about Dixie and doing something with her that evening, but Dixie's sister was housebound a couple of towns over, and Dixie had gone to spend the evening with her.

Normally that would make Joanna happy, because she and Stonewall would have a few hours to themselves. Not that they were going to do anything. They'd just hang out, play games, or maybe even take a drive, but most likely they'd just work on the house. Whatever they did would be casual and fun.

But now, she wasn't sure. She hadn't talked to him since he got back. Maybe he was taking Whitney out again and that's where he had gone. It was just very much unlike him not to say something to her first. But, like he said, that wasn't her position in his life anymore, and she needed to get used to it.

She spent the afternoon working in the upstairs bedroom. Declan and Stonewall had put a huge master closet in the upstairs master bedroom. Joanna had to admit it was a closet that would make any woman happy. And they'd done an excellent job. She had been touching up the paint and painting the baseboards for them to put on.

After that, they needed to put the light fixtures and shelving in, and it would be finished.

She moseyed up to the top of the stairs, wondering if she should double-check that all the pizza was put away when the front door opened, and Whitney stepped in, laughing, followed by Stonewall, who must have just said something funny because he had a grin on his face.

Joanna remembered those days. They weren't that far away, where they were laughing and joking with each other. Stonewall had an amazing sense of humor. She wasn't sure what she liked better about him, that sense of humor or his intelligence. Or maybe it was his strength of character. Probably that.

She gave a weak smile and said, "Good evening," before she turned around and walked back to the bedroom.

She probably should have told Stonewall that she noticed that the closet door had a tendency to stick. He needed to shave just a little bit more off the top or the bottom, or maybe both. She'd barely gotten it open when she tried to shut it earlier. But she didn't want to go back out and talk to them. She would give them all the time they needed, because that's what she had told Miss Dixie that she would do, and she did truly want Stonewall to be happy.

Then, footsteps on the stairs almost caused her to try to duck into the closet and hide.

Instead, she grabbed her paintbrush which she had set down and started painting the last of the trim.

"Joanna, there you are," Whitney said.

Joanna swallowed down the lump that seemed to be lodged in her chest before she turned, carefully putting a smile on her face and aiming it at Whitney. "Sounds like you've been having a good time."

"I had a great day," Whitney said. "I did want to talk to you and Stonewall, and I keep hearing about this huge closet. I want to see it."

"You want to talk to us?" Joanna said, wondering what in the world she could possibly want to talk to them about.

"I do. You can wait for a couple of minutes, though, right?" She looked back. "Stonewall? Are you going to show this monstrous thing to me that you said any woman would fall in love with?"

"That wasn't what I said. That was what Joanna said."

"I wasn't talking to you when I said that," Joanna said before she could think. She had been talking to Miss Dixie last night and hadn't realized Stonewall had been listening.

"That was the quote from you anyway," Stonewall said, although the smile faded from his face as though he felt like she was censuring him for quoting her or something.

She didn't mean to.

In order to try to make up for it, she said, "It's right here. And it really is huge. Stonewall and Declan did a great job on it." She said that without any jealousy at all. And she was almost happy. After all, Whitney was getting a really great guy, and she felt Whitney was a wonderful woman for Stonewall. Why wasn't she happier for them? If she loved Stonewall as she thought she did, shouldn't she be happy that he found someone wonderful? Why did it hurt so much?

Whitney trailed her over to the closet, and she looked back over her shoulder at Stonewall. "She said you were the one who made it? Aren't you going to give me the grand tour?"

With Whitney standing so close, Joanna needed to move into the closet, but she really didn't want to be in there while Stonewall walked around. He had made a cute little shoe rack for shoes, and the lighting that he was going to install was going to be spectacular. There was also a huge floor-to-ceiling mirror which was placed at a perfect angle.

"Well, it's like this," Stonewall started, and Joanna turned away. His voice, so familiar, so beloved, wrapped around her spine and settled in her stomach like warm honey. She wanted to hold it close to her, but she knew it was just a matter of time before it was a voice that she did not hear every day, probably not every week, maybe not even every year.

Despite herself, she wrapped her arms around her stomach and pretended to study a spot on the wall.

She wasn't looking at the door when she heard it slam shut and Stonewall say, "What—?"

She spun around, using the light from the work light to see Stonewall standing there staring at the closed door. Whitney was nowhere in sight.

She heard something being dragged on the floor, and then something else being shoved underneath the doorknob as Stonewall rattled it, trying to turn and push it.

"I meant to tell you that it stuck," Joanna said, realizing that he was trying to open the door but still not quite figuring out what had happened.

"Whitney? What's going on? Why did you slam the door so hard? I think it's jammed."

"Yeah. I think it's jammed too. And I also have something sitting here in front of it that will hopefully keep it from un-jamming very easily."

"Why? What's going on?" Stonewall said again.

He seemed just as confused as Joanna felt, which somehow helped ease her mind and made her feel better. She wasn't the only one in the dark.

"You and Joanna need to figure things out. Both of you are in love with each other, and both of you need to stop pussyfooting around and tell the other one. And while you're at it, you need to try some kissing too." Joanna could almost see Whitney nodding her head, stomping her foot, and then spinning on her toes.

"I will be back in the morning with someone who can open that door. In the meantime, you two stay put and get things worked out. And I mean it."

For good measure, she must have slammed the bedroom door, and then they faintly heard stomping down the steps, and then the front door opened and closed, leaving them completely alone and stuck in the closet together.

Chapter Twenty-Six

S tonewall stood and stared at the closet door. He was pretty sure he could get the thing open. All it would take would be for him to ram his shoulder into it a few times while Joanna made sure that the doorknob was twisted so it didn't catch.

But... He kind of liked this idea. He had to hand it to Whitney, she sure knew how to pull the rug out from under someone. And she had been using her schoolteacher voice, which was very authoritative. He had to tell her that the next time he saw her. He hoped to be thanking her too. Because she did what he had wanted to do. Only she did it a little bit before he wanted to, but his mom shouldn't find out considering that she wasn't home.

He shoved any thoughts of his mother out of his head. Joanna was here, and Whitney was right. He needed to level with her.

He tried not to focus on the kissing part, because he felt like that was a pretty good idea too.

"It's jammed pretty tight," Stonewall said slowly as he turned to look at Joanna.

She nodded, not acknowledging at all what Whitney said. Stonewall was still going over it in his mind. He supposed that his feelings had been looming large, but come to think of it, Whitney had said that

Joanna was in love with him the same as she said that he was in love with her. He was pretty sure Whitney was right about him, but what he really wanted to find out was if she was right about Joanna.

But what Caleb had said ran through his mind. It wasn't right for him to expect Joanna to bare her feelings first. He was the man. He was the one who was supposed to be brave and take chances and be the one who blazed the trail. Even if sometimes that trail led to embarrassment for him.

Did he want to spend the rest of the night with Joanna if he admitted that he loved her and she didn't return his feelings?

He wasn't even going to entertain that thought.

"So did you and Whitney have a nice afternoon?" Joanna said, like Whitney hadn't said anything.

He ground his back teeth together. He supposed if it had been him, and Joanna had been going out on dates for the last three weekends with some other guy, and he hadn't heard anything about what had happened, and then she had disappeared for a while and walked back in with that guy, yeah, he supposed he would want to have a little bit of an explanation before he felt safe to talk about feelings.

Not that he enjoyed talking about feelings, like, ever. But he was going to do it tonight. If Joanna allowed him to. She didn't look very happy right now. And normally, that type of attitude was never directed at him. He definitely did not like that.

"I didn't spend the afternoon with Whitney. I met her as we were coming up the front porch steps together."

"Really?" Joanna said, and he didn't get the feeling that she didn't believe him. He had the feeling that she was asking where he was.

"I had walked to the playground so that I could call your brother Caleb."

"Caleb?" she asked, furrowing her brows and probably wondering why in the world he would have needed to walk to the playground to call Caleb.

"I was trying to call Ezra, but Ezra didn't answer. So I figured I would call Caleb next. And he answered on the first ring."

"I see." But it was plain that she didn't.

"I have a problem, and I wanted to ask someone older and a little wiser than me what to do."

"I see," she said, putting her hands over her chest and leaning back against the wall.

He shoved a hand in his pocket and put a hand on the doorjamb, leaning on it, wanting to close the distance between them, knowing that he needed to say a few things first. And maybe never.

"What was your problem?" she asked, and she sounded guarded like there was still a wall between them.

He was hoping he could talk that wall down. But he didn't really have the confidence he could. He was just going to try and hope for the best.

"Well, I've gone on three dates with Whitney, and..." He paused. Her eyes had added more space between them without moving at all. Maybe he shouldn't have started out talking about Whitney, but hopefully she would understand when he said this next sentence.

"I don't feel anything for her. Nothing. And yet, my best friend and my mom seem to keep continuously pushing me into her. But after going on three dates with her, I realized that there is someone else I want."

"You don't want Whitney?" she asked, so she was still processing that part.

"I don't want Whitney. I shouldn't want Whitney, I can't possibly want Whitney when every time I'm with Whitney, I can't stop thinking about you."

That was hard, and a part of him felt like his whole insides were dropping out and falling, falling without hitting anything and just falling.

But that wasn't nearly all he had to say.

She didn't have anything to say to that; she just looked confused.

"I was at the playground, talking to your brother, and I thought about kids. I never think about kids. But... I thought about coming to the playground with kids, yours and mine. And how much I thought I would enjoy that."

Still wasn't what he wanted to say. They could have been her kids with someone else and his kids with someone else. Man, he should have thought about this a little bit before he started talking.

"I want us to have children together."

No. That was not a good place to start either.

Her eyes got big. So now she definitely understood what he was trying to get at, even if it came out from the completely wrong side.

"Joanna, you've been my best friend forever. Since we came here, my feelings for you have changed. I... I feel like I want to touch you. Kiss you. Be more with you. And so I told Whitney... Whitney and I decided that yesterday would be our last date. We felt like we had made enough of an effort to appease my mother and that we can honestly say that it just wasn't working out. We knew it from the beginning though. Because... It's pretty obvious to everyone that you're the only one for me." He saw her throat move. She was swallowing hard, but she hadn't moved at all. She leaned against the wall, still looked at him, and he still felt like there was a wall between them. Should he give her time to process? Or should he push harder?

He dropped his arm from the doorframe and took a step toward her. Then another. He lifted his hand, and for the first time, he touched her face in a gentle caress. The caress of a man who loved a woman, not the caress of a friend.

"I don't want to live without you. I was hoping that maybe you might possibly learn to feel the same way about me. Not as a friend. As...a lover. A husband."

Her breath seemed to be coming in shallow pants as she looked up at him, but she still hadn't said anything, and while he remained hopeful, he was trying to steel himself against how embarrassing it was going to be if she told him to back off.

"Joanna. You're scaring me," he said. His other hand came up, wrapping around her face and pulling her away from the wall and toward him. The hand that had been on her cheek wrapped around her neck, and she allowed him to tilt her head so that she was looking up at him.

"If you don't say something soon, I'm going to kiss you."

That made her smile, but it didn't make her say anything, and maybe he could read her just as well as he always had, because he could tell from the expression on her face that she wasn't going to say anything, just so that he would kiss her.

"You little imp. How long have you known that you wanted me too?"

Her smile grew broader. "Since we came here. It took you long enough. Two weeks. Man. Are you always going to move this slow?"

He laughed, and he lowered his head, and their breath mingled as their mouths touched, and he realized the kissing thing with his best friend was a lot better than he had thought it might be.

He really didn't want to stop, but they were stuck in a closet, and he figured he ought to have at least a little semblance of self-control. Plus, she hadn't said anything.

He brought his thumb up and caressed her cheek as his lips touched her forehead. "I love you. I think I always have."

Her arms had circled his waist; now they moved up his back as her lips settled on his chin. "I love you too. And the same. Since I saw you. I think that's when I started to love you."

"I guess I'm not the only one who moves kind of slow around here," he said, and he felt the puff of her breath against his neck.

"Don't you have anything to say?" he finally asked.

"I've been through the ringer. I thought I lost you. I thought I had to let you go. I thought I was getting ready to prepare myself to never hear your voice again, to have to look at you with someone else and be okay with it, and now I'm the one you're with, and I can't hardly believe it. Can you give me a little bit of time to get used to it, because this is hard."

"Take all the time you want. Looks like a good thing." He paused and then figured he could confess, "I'm pretty sure I can get the door open."

"I know you can," she said, and he had to smile. It sounded just like Joanna. She believed he could do anything, and she hadn't been fooled by the door for one second.

"But I do think it was pretty clever on Whitney's part," she added, her hands going out to play with the hair at the base of his neck. He really liked that and didn't want to move.

Could they confess their love for each other, decide they wanted to be romantic partners, and could he ask her to marry her on the same night?

It was kind of tempting.

But that thought flew out of the window when she said, "How do we break this to your mom?"

Oh yeah. He'd forgotten about that.

"Do we have to think about that right now? Can I just bask in the glow of finally holding you and knowing that everything's going to be okay? You realize that this has been in my head for the last couple of weeks and I've been too scared to do anything about it?"

"You and me both. I was too scared too. I... I was afraid that if I did, I would ruin everything."

"Me too. That was my biggest fear, that and that you didn't seem to care for me at all. You seemed to be stiff-arming me every time I tried to bring it up."

"You tried to bring it up?" she asked, pulling back just a little and looking at him.

"I dropped little hints here and there. You know, you weren't your usual intuitive self. Typically, I don't even have to drop anything and you're on me like a fly on honey."

"Fly. Really? That's the best you can do?"

"I guess I probably ought to think about some more compliments for you. I mean, considering that I kind of enjoy kissing you and I want to get to do it more."

She laughed. "You don't have to compliment me to kiss me. I mean, it's nice and everything, but it's not a necessity."

"I think it is," he said, brushing the hair back away from her face and smiling down into her eyes. He couldn't believe how much better he felt having just said what they said. It felt like all the pieces had clicked into place and his whole being was aligned with hers. And he couldn't imagine how things could get better.

But his mother might be a problem.

"Things just didn't work out between Whitney and me. She's a nice girl and everything, but she's just not you. I don't know if my mom can accept that or not, and I hope you're okay with it if she doesn't."

"I'll be sad, for sure. I...really like her, which is a surprise. I wasn't expecting to like her. I just thought I would try to get her to like me. She's a nice lady. And she knows a lot. I just...know that she had her heart set on you and Whitney."

"Should we tell her tomorrow after church?"

"She's gonna want to know why you and Whitney aren't together."

"I want to go to church and hold your hand, put my arm around you, snuggle. That will definitely make the service a lot more enjoyable."

"That's not the purpose of church," she said, and he grinned. She was right. Still, he had a girl now, and he wanted the world to know it.

"Can we tell her before church?" he asked hopefully.

"I suppose if we get up early enough. But it might be nicer to go to church with her happy and then give her the afternoon to get over it."

"You seem sure that she's not going to be happy about us."

"I don't know. I haven't heard her say a word about you and me. I have a feeling she's not going to be thrilled that Whitney isn't in the picture anymore and she's going to blame me."

"We'll just see about that." He thought, he could be wrong, but he thought that maybe his mom felt the same way about Joanna that Joanna felt about her. And that was all because of Joanna taking the time to try to win her over.

Chapter Twenty-Seven

"I can get that. You go ahead and sit down," Joanna said as she took the oven mitts from Miss Dixie. Church had gone well, and Stonewall had arrived early, but neither one of them had wanted to make waves this morning. So now, they were sitting down for the meatloaf and mashed potatoes that Dixie and she had made, and from the look on Stonewall's face, he was determined to pray and then launch into the subject that he most wanted to talk about.

Joanna gave him a shy smile behind Miss Dixie's back. She had been a little disappointed when they hadn't discussed anything before church. He was right about wanting to hold his hand and sit with his arm around her. Even though she had said that that wasn't what church was for, it was what being with someone was all about. Feeling comfortable with them and able to touch them anytime a person wanted to.

She couldn't wait until she could do that with Stonewall. She wasn't sure exactly what had shifted, because he was still the man who had always been her best friend, but now it was even better.

She said a silent prayer thanking God for working everything out. And praying that this conversation would go as smoothly as possible. She wasn't sure that Miss Dixie would be happy that Stonewall was going to end up with her instead of Whitney. In fact, she half expected Miss Dixie to feel betrayed that Joanna had somehow slipped in unaware and stolen Stonewall away from Whitney.

They settled into their chairs, and Stonewall said a short prayer. Before they'd even passed anything, he said, "Mom, there's something I need to tell you."

"My goodness. You sound so serious," she said. Then she looked around the table. "Does this have to do with Whitney?" She sounded so hopeful, Joanna's heart fell.

"A little bit. I guess it does. Because Whitney and I decided after three dates and trying as hard as we could, that there was just nothing between us."

"Oh no," Miss Dixie said, setting the potatoes that she held onto the table as though they were just too heavy for her to continue to hold in her disappointed state.

"But you are going to see me get married before you die, because Whitney shoved Joanna and me in a closet last night and told us to not leave it until we got things settled between us." Stonewall paused just for a moment but not long enough for his mother to say anything. "We figured out that we are in love. And I'm going to ask her to marry me just as soon as I think she'll say yes."

Joanna wanted to butt into that conversation and say, "I'd say yes right now," but she didn't. She was watching Miss Dixie.

"Whitney shoved you two into a closet?"

"In the rental where we're working. And yes. Whitney did it. She and I had already decided that the two of us were not going to work out."

"So you did. I see." Miss Dixie looked at him, and then she looked at Joanna. Joanna expected her eyes to narrow and for her to look angry, but they softened instead. "You know what, I would be ecstatic to have you as a daughter-in-law. I didn't realize what an amazing person you are. But now I can understand why my son has loved you for so long. I love you too."

Joanna knew her mouth was opening and closing like a fish, but she couldn't stop it.

It took her a bit to find her voice. "Wow! That's awesome. I don't have a mom, and I've learned so much from you. I was afraid you were going to be upset with me."

"No. I can see how much my son admires and respects you. And like I said, I understand why now. I just hope you two will let me be a part of your lives. I could have done better by my son when I was raising him, and maybe part of my problem is that I feel guilty about it. I feel guilty that he went to you, when I didn't give him the attention that he needed."

"Don't beat yourself up about it, Mom. I kinda feel like it all worked out for good, and you are absolutely welcome to be a part of our lives. In fact, it would be really awesome if you moved to North Dakota."

"I couldn't do that."

"We can always use help on the ranch, and with the dude ranch, there is definitely room for a good cook." Joanna said that with confidence. It seemed like there was always stuff to do and never enough help.

"I'll have to think about that, but it's tempting. After all, you're my only child and it's lonely here without you. Of course, with my sister here in Wyoming, I might not want to leave her."

"Bring her with you," Joanna said easily.

"But she needs to be taken care of. It's not going to be long until she's going to need more than a little bit of help."

"There are plenty of people on the farm to help. But she needs to do what's best for her, and you need to make the best decision for you. We don't want to talk you into anything that you would regret." Stonewall looked across the table and smiled at Joanna. She agreed with him completely, and he could see on her face that she was sure.

He could also see that she would be happy to marry him today. If he couldn't, he couldn't read her as well as what she thought.

But there would be plenty of time to talk about that. Later.

Chapter Twenty-Eight

"I can't believe you guys are really leaving," Declan said as he picked up another piece of pizza from the box and shoved half of it in his mouth.

"The house looks awesome. You guys have been a great help," Stonewall said, his arm around Joanna, holding her close. He couldn't believe that he'd spent so much time standing a foot apart from her when he could have her tucked against him like this. He didn't think he ever wanted to be apart from her again.

She might have a different idea, but so far, she seemed to be pretty happy snuggled up with him.

Maybe it would get old for her, but he didn't think the newness and the happiness of having her with him would ever wear off for him. After all, he'd never gotten tired of having her around as a friend and in fact felt lonely and unsettled when she wasn't around. He knew that, after the two weeks he spent trying to get interested in Whitney.

"How's your business coming?" Joanna asked, once Declan had chewed enough to answer.

"I think it's going pretty good. I've got some friends helping me, and thanks to the things we learned from you guys, we can do a lot of handiwork."

"I can help too!" Lolly said, coming over to grab another piece of pizza. Lolly had become a regular just like the teenagers, and Joanna hoped that maybe her life would take a slightly different direction than what it previously had been going. She actually seemed to have taken a shine to Miss Dixie, who was supposed to come along a little later with a chocolate cake that she had insisted on baking.

"I have some news," Whitney said, coming over and ruffling Lolly's hair before looking at Joanna and Stonewall.

Stonewall's arm tightened around Joanna, but he didn't have to say anything.

"You do? That sounds exciting." Joanna sounded truly interested and happy.

"It is. I got the principal position at Sweet Water High. I'll be there next September."

"Wow. Congratulations."

"That's great," Stonewall echoed Joanna's praise. Grateful that things had worked out well, and they'd ended on good terms. It would be a little awkward to have her in the same small town if they hadn't.

Maybe after she came, she would find someone who suited her a little better than he did.

"I hope you two are going to invite me to your wedding."

There was silence for a moment, and then Joanna said, "He hasn't asked me yet. But if I have anything to do with it, you're definitely invited."

"He hasn't asked you yet? You guys got out of the closet way too soon," Whitney said, and they all laughed together.

Stonewall waited for them to finish talking and for Whitney to walk away.

"I haven't found a ring that suits you. But I am going to ask you, and it's going to be soon."

"I don't need a ring. I don't care about that. I just want you," she whispered back, lifting her head up so that her words hit his neck and made his skin tingle.

He loved that. And he knew it was true. She really didn't care about that stuff, she only cared about him. That's the way it had always been with them. And as far as he could tell, it's the way it would always be.

"Then let's plan on it. Marry me, because I can't live without you."

"I'll marry you, because I can't live without you," she said, emphasizing the change in her sentence.

He smiled, pulling her close and wishing there weren't so many people around, because kissing Joanna was a lot better than being her best friend.

Chapter Twenty-Nine

"That might be their headlights, there." Ezra sat on the porch swing beside his wife, a blanket thrown over them to keep out the chill of the early spring evening, watching the light in the distance as it grew brighter.

"Were they coming here to see us before they went home?" Alaska asked, her side pressed against his, a hand on his leg under the blanket. Her fingers had been making lazy circles over his jeans, and he'd been enjoying her gentle touch.

"Yes. Joanna had something she wanted to tell us, and she didn't want to wait until tomorrow."

"Do you think—?" Alaska's voice held hope and excitement.

"I'm hoping, but I didn't want to get your hopes up," he said, gazing down at her and allowing her to see the love in his eyes. Nothing was more important to him than loving and protecting his family, all of his family, but that started with the small woman beside him. God had given him exactly what he needed, and he intended to do his very best to love her like Christ loved the church and gave himself for it. He failed every day, but he also tried with all his heart every day as well.

"You were probably wise to be cautious, because now I'm so excited I can hardly sit still. Maybe they've figured out that they're perfect for each other and...maybe they've gotten married while they've been away!"

"I don't think they went that far." But he could be wrong, and his wife could be right. In their family, they had a tendency to be very low-key about weddings. Not only because they'd not had much extra income to "waste" on a big celebration, but also because their family just wasn't the kind of family to throw a pile of money around on a big show.

The headlights were definitely getting closer. They were going to find out very soon what Joanna wanted to tell them.

"Did you hear who got the principal position at Sweet Water High?" His wife's fingers had started their lazy circles again. Ezra closed his eyes.

"I did." He might have had a little something to do with that, too. He wasn't on the board, but he knew people who knew people, and he didn't hesitate to put in a good word for someone he knew would make a great principal. She would also make one of his brothers a great wife.

"You sly stinker! You knew! You probably knew she applied and put in a word for her."

"Maybe." He grinned without opening his eyes. As the oldest of his family and as the man responsible for his siblings, it was his job to know and do things like that.

"So...what are you going to do?"

"I'm going to see what Joanna has to say. Then, if I like what I hear, I think there might be a certain woman who's going to need a little help cleaning up her house and moving, and I have a brother who would just love to drive back to Wyoming to help with that."

"Oh, he would?"

"He might not know it, but yes, he would."

"What about Priscilla?"

His heart stumbled. Priscilla deserved so much more than what she'd gotten. He wanted to make everything right with her, but so far, God had other plans for her life, and God's plans were always far superior to Ezra's. Even when they hurt. Everything would work out for Priscilla's good and God's glory in the end. But so far, her story had been painful.

"She's going back to Wyoming to be with her kids."

"I thought she accepted your offer of the high-dollar lawyer."

"She did. But she's going back in the meantime."

Headlights flashed across the yard as a small, sweet-smelling breeze flowed over the porch, chilly but holding the promise of new life and new beginnings.

The motor cut and Stonewall got out, throwing up a hand in a wave as he walked around the front of the truck to open the passenger door.

"He's opening her door!" Alaska hissed with barely suppressed excitement, like Ezra couldn't see that and know the implications for himself. He smiled to his soul. His sister and her best friend had figured out what the rest of the world had known for a very long time.

Stonewall held a hand out and Joanna took it, sliding out of his truck and smiling up into his eyes. They paused for a moment as though speaking, although they said no words, before turning toward the house and walking to the porch.

"Good evening," Stonewall said, keeping Joanna's hand tucked into his. Ezra did not miss the way he put his other hand over top of hers and held it tight against him.

"It's a nice evening," Ezra said, wanting the small talk to be over so they could find out exactly where things stood. Then, he wanted to take his own wife inside and make sure she knew exactly how much he loved and treasured her.

"We wanted to let you know that Joanna and I have decided to get married." Stonewall paused. "I suppose I should ask your permission, but I have the feeling you gave it long ago."

"That's correct. Joanna couldn't have found a better man. I always thought God sent you to us."

"I agree," Joanna said with a grin at Stonewall before she slipped from his side and came over and hugged first Ezra then Alaska. "Thank you for modeling what a good marriage looks like."

Ezra hugged her back but could not take credit for his marriage. "That's all God."

His wife gave him a look that said she gave him credit too, but she didn't contradict him.

"When is the wedding?" she asked as Joanna moved back to

Stonewall's side and he slid an arm around her, pulling her close, like he couldn't stand to be separated from her for even that long.

"This week if we can fit it in the schedule. We haven't talked to the preacher, so whenever it will work for him and for you, we're going to jump on it."

Ezra smiled as they talked a bit about the things that women always fussed over—food and clothes and decorations.

"My mom is coming tomorrow, and I thought it would be okay for her to live on Joanna's side of the duplex, since Joanna is moving in with me."

"That's fine, of course." Ezra always figured it was good to have family around as much as possible.

"And do you remember Whitney Singleton? The woman my mom was trying to set me up with? She went to our church in Wyoming."

"I remember," he said, trying not to hold his breath.

"She's going to be the new principal this coming fall at Sweet Water High. I told her she might be able to get a job here on the ranch over the summer and that we'd help her get settled and maybe find a place for her to stay until she finds a place of her own?"

"Absolutely." Ezra felt a deep sense of rightness settle down into his soul. If things went well, another one of his brothers would be getting married before the end of the year. It was shaping up to be a very, very good year. If only God would work things out with Priscilla. But they would get worked out—in God's time and not one second before. Ezra knew that as sure as he knew God was good. All the time.

It was another ten or fifteen minutes before Joanna and Stonewall said good night and headed back down the road.

"Are you ready to head to bed, love?" Ezra murmured in Alaska's ear before he nuzzled her temple and placed a light kiss there.

"Always," she breathed. Her fingers had moved slightly, and he barely remembered to grab the blanket as they stood and walked in the house together.

∿

Join Jessie's list and be the first to know about new releases and sales on her books!

Read *A Cowboy's Whispered Word*, a tender installment in the Sweet View Ranch series in which Whitney returns to the small town of her childhood—and to the cowboy who once changed everything with a single whispered word. He doesn't remember, but she never forgot. Now it might be her turn to show him what it means to be fearless... and maybe, just maybe, finally share the truth that's been in her heart for twenty years.

Sneek Peek of A Cowboy's Whispered Word

12 years ago

Whitney Singleton sat on a branch under low-hanging leaves near the playground of her hometown of Wild, Wyoming. Her face was streaked with tears, but under the canopy of the sheltering tree, no passerby would notice.

No passerby would notice her, for that matter. She was off to the side of the playground, and there shouldn't be any people passing by.

Not that she cared. She had come here for privacy, yes, but she was swallowed up by grief and fear.

Her parents had been married for twenty years before she had been born. She suspected, although they never said, that they had decided not to have children and then changed their minds when it was almost too late.

Maybe that wasn't the way it went, but she often imagined that it was. Regardless, her mother was in her late sixties, and her dad was seventy. Far, far older than any of her classmates' parents.

It hadn't bothered her that much. Sometimes when they went on vacation, people asked her if she enjoyed going with her grandparents or if her grandmother wanted this or that.

When she was younger, she had thought it was funny that they thought that her parents were her grandparents. As she grew older, now being the ripe old age of twelve, she knew that her parents were just a lot older than other people's parents and it was a natural mistake.

She was different.

But today her parents had sat down when she got home from school and given her the news: her mother had cancer.

Her mother had been all smiles, pretending that it wasn't that big of a deal, that the C word didn't strike fear into the hearts of anyone who heard it. Whether it was about oneself or one's loved ones.

Her father had said that they would fight it. That their doctors were very good, even though the hospital was rural, and that they had caught it early, and that her mother had a very high chance of surviving for five years.

Did they not realize that in five years she would only be seventeen? She wouldn't even have graduated from high school.

She wanted her parents with her all of her life, not...for less than half of it.

Why, Lord? Why did You give me to parents who aren't going to be here to raise me? And why don't I have siblings? Other people who I can depend on?

It was just her and her parents. Her parents' parents were long since gone. Her dad had a brother, although she didn't know where he was and didn't know much about him. He had a family of his own; she'd seen him once or twice at Christmas throughout her childhood.

Her mother had a brother too, and it was the same deal. She knew about him, had seen his family, met her cousins, but they weren't close.

They lived in a different state, and she wasn't even sure which one.

Up until this point in time, she had been lonely at times but hadn't really thought about the implications of not having much family. But if her mother died, and her dad died, she would be...alone.

A shout and some scuffling brought her head up, trying to make sure that no one had discovered her hiding spot.

No, just the Clyborne family playing a game of basketball on the court fifty yards away.

Everyone knew the Clybornes. Who didn't know of a family with twelve children? They were certain to garner attention wherever they went.

They were homeschooled, although they went to her church. She knew some of the younger siblings, although she and her family didn't go religiously the way the Clybornes did. But everyone knew that there were twelve of them and that their parents had died in a car accident. The older siblings were raising the younger ones, and the whole family stuck together.

She could understand why God would take the parents of a family like that. They all had each other to lean on.

She watched as one of the older boys dribbled to the basket.

She didn't recognize that one, but one who was slightly taller, slightly broader of the shoulder, the one who always had a smile on his face, caught her eye.

Caleb. She knew Caleb Clyborne. He sold goat milk to her family and delivered it once a week. He'd been doing it for the last six years, although he had told her parents that one of his younger siblings was going to be taking over his route soon, since he was getting into other things, and up until that point, that had been the biggest blow of Whitney's young life.

After all, she had made sure that she was around every Thursday afternoon when Caleb delivered his milk.

Her parents were rather old-fashioned and preferred the unpasteurized goat milk to the store-bought homogenized, pasteurized, and "dead" stuff, as her dad called it. He had grown up on a dairy farm, and while he would prefer cow milk, anything that hadn't been tampered with by the government, according to him, was better than what a person could buy in the store.

Whitney didn't care. She just loved seeing Caleb. He always had a smile and a gleam in his eye.

Of course, he was much, much older than she was and didn't even know she was alive.

If she had calculated correctly, he was exactly twice as old as she was, and while she suspected that it was normal for a girl her age to crush on a much older man, she also knew that there was no way that the man was going to notice her, and if he did, he wouldn't do anything about it. He couldn't. She was too young.

Life was so unfair.

The idea brought a fresh round of tears, and she buried her head in her arms which lay on the tree branch near her forehead. Her mother had cancer and was going to die, the boy she liked was too old for her, he had never noticed her, and even if he did, he would never wait for her. It would be at least six years before she was old enough, and her parents had been emphatic that she go to college and get some kind of degree. They didn't care what—it could be a BS in basket weaving for all they cared—but she had no choice. She was going to college.

What did it matter if she went to college if she wasn't going to have a mother?

She pitied herself for a bit and then realized that Caleb didn't have a mother either, and he would understand. Except... It wasn't like he was going to talk to her or anything.

She tried to wipe away her tears and dry her cheeks so she could walk back home and no one would know that she had been crying, but fresh tears started before she could even get the old ones dried off.

She just needed to stay here for a bit and cry herself out. Her parents would be able to tell that she was upset, and they would understand too.

But there was nothing they could say that would make it any better.

Sign up for Jessie's newsletter! Get a free book, access to exclusive bonus content, get fun and funny updates on her life on the farm and more!

A Gift from Jessie

View this code through your smart phone camera to be taken to a page where you can download a FREE ebook when you sign up to get updates from Jessie Gussman! Find out why people say, "Jessie's is the only newsletter I open and read" and "You make my day brighter. Love, love, love reading your newsletters. I don't know where you find time to write books. You are so busy living life. A true blessing." and "I know from now on that I can't be drinking my morning coffee while reading your newsletter – I laughed so hard I sprayed it out all over the table!"

Claim your free book from Jessie!

Escape to more faith-filled romance series by Jessie Gussman!

The Complete Sweet Water, North Dakota Reading Order:

Series One: Sweet Water Ranch Western Cowboy Romance (11 book series)

Series Two: Coming Home to North Dakota (12 book series)

Series Three: Flyboys of Sweet Briar Ranch in North Dakota (13 book series)

Series Four: Sweet View Ranch Western Cowboy Romance (10 book series)

Spinoffs and More! Additional Series You'll Love:

Jessie's First Series: Sweet Haven Farm (4 book series)

Small-Town Romance: The Baxter Boys (5 book series)

Bad-Boy Sweet Romance: Richmond Rebels Sweet Romance (3 book series)

Sweet Water Spinoff: Cowboy Crossing (9 book series)

Small Town Romantic Comedy: Good Grief, Idaho (5 book series)

True Stories from Jessie's Farm: Stories from Jessie Gussman's Newsletter (3 book series)

Reader-Favorite! Sweet Beach Romance: Blueberry Beach (8 book series)

Blueberry Beach Spinoff: Strawberry Sands (10 book series)

From Strawberry Sands to: Raspberry Ridge (12 book series)

Swoonfully Jolly Holiday Stories:

Holiday Romance: Cowboy Mountain Christmas (6 book series)

Cowboy Mountain Christmas Spinoff: A Heartland Cowboy Christmas (9 book series)

New and Much Loved: Mistletoe Meadows (4 books and counting!)

Laughing Through the Snow: Christmas Tree, PA Sweet Romcoms (6 short reads)

www.ingramcontent.com/pod-product-compliance
Lightning Source LLC
Chambersburg PA
CBHW060328260626
47160CB00007B/2721